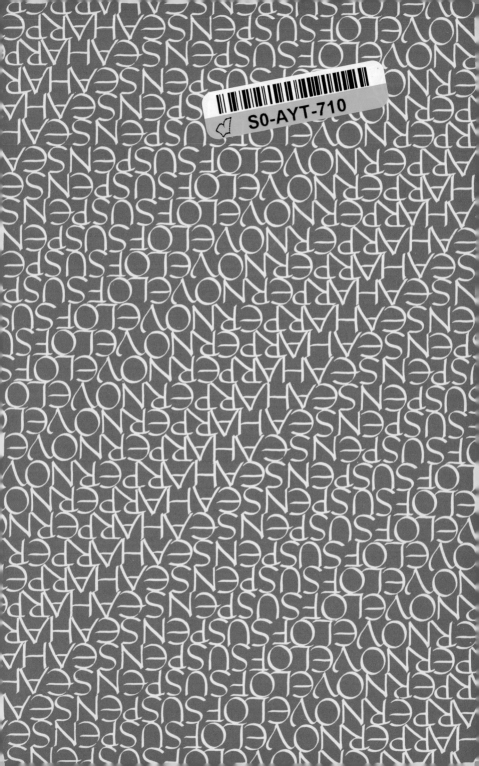

The Kama Sutra Tango

A JOAN KAHN BOOK

BOOKS BY J. F. BURKE

The Kama Sutra Tango

J. F. Burke

HARPER & ROW, PUBLISHERS
NEW YORK, HAGERSTOWN, SAN FRANCISCO, LONDON

A HARPER NOVEL OF SUSPENSE

FIRST EDITION

Designed by Gloria Adelson

Library of Congress Cataloging in Publication Data

Burke, J.F., date
  The kama sutra tango.
  I. Title.
PZ3.B91567Kam   [PS3503.U6126]   813'.5'4   76–47257
ISBN 0–06–010569–0

77 78 79 80 10 9 8 7 6 5 4 3 2 1

For C. R. C.

The Kama Sutra Tango

❦ 1 ❧

IT WAS MIDNIGHT. I had just finished a set of Ellington show tunes, and it was time for my break. So I closed the piano lid, took a bow, and retired to the employees' rest rooms. I was feeling good. We had a nice crowd, every table occupied, guests waiting three deep at the bar. And my favorite ballerina, the lithe and lissome Victoria Moorcroft, had phoned the night before saying she'd be flying in tonight from Chicago and staying with me a whole week. She and I hadn't been together in more than a month. I lit an eighty-five-cent Brazilian cigar.

I was standing in front of the urinal, listening to voices in the patio. The window was open, for it was a balmy early-spring night and there was no air conditioning in the john. I heard the heavy Sicilian accent of Jock Alfieri, my business partner, co-owner of Pal Joey's. He was talking with a man whose tight Irish tenor I knew well, Mike Maginnis, a lieutenant in the Eighteenth Precinct, nowadays called Midtown North. I wondered what he was

1

doing here, since his regular payday was the first of the month and this was the seventeenth.

"More," he was saying. "More, Jock, a lot more."

Jock laughed good-naturedly. He was an amiable man. He laughed at just about everything. I used to tell him he'd die laughing.

"Hey, Mike!" he said. "You getting a grand a month now, right?"

"It ought to be a grand a week," Maginnis said. "It's cut too many ways, Jock. A grand a week wouldn't be a lot— very small potatoes, in fact."

"Not so small," Jock said. "How about every *two* weeks, Mike? I gotta talk to Joe. You come see me tomorrow, okay?"

Jock was stalling. He didn't have to talk to me about raising Maginnis's payoff, if that's what he wanted to do, because I always stayed as far away from the business end of the club as I could. I let him and Charlie Green, our lawyer-accountant, handle the financial details.

Maginnis said, "Hell, no! We talk to Streeter tonight, right now, while he's taking his break. You don't hear no piano in there, do you? So get him out here."

I zippered my fly and stepped over to the open window. Jock's back was to me, but Maginnis could see me. His little pig eyes flared when I appeared in the window, but he said nothing. Then his eyes moved slightly, looking past Jock.

I followed his gaze and saw someone coming out of the shadows to the right, stepping into the shaft of light from the window. What I saw—or rather, what I thought I saw, for the light was poor and the action happened very fast —was a small, slim man in a broad-brimmed gray fedora and a tight-fitting dark-blue suit with sharp shoulders and wide lapels. He carried an automatic pistol, and he was pointing it at Jock's back.

I shouted, "Jock! Look out! Behind you!"

Maginnis crouched low. Jock turned, smiling, and got the bullet in his face. He fell backward. The shot sounded like a cannon, and it blew off the top of his head and splattered his brains all over the patio wall.

Maginnis had scurried away, heading for the narrow alley to the left, between our building and the next one. The gunman shifted fast on his feet and pointed the gun at my window. I got a good look at him: young, soft lines to the face, small jaw, black rat's-tail mustache, a little black goatee, long black sideburns, and large pink sunglasses. I also noticed black gloves. I thought the gun was a Luger type.

I ducked below the window sill, and when the second shot didn't come I raised up slightly and peered over the ledge. There was nobody in the patio but Jock. I heard the rusty squeak of the fire escape ladder.

I ran down the hall, past the dressing rooms, through the kitchen, and out into the patio. Jock lay on his back in a puddle of blood. I looked up and saw the gunman climbing the fire escape, silhouetted against the red glow of the night sky over Times Square. He was already at the third floor. I could never catch him, for there were several ways he could go across the roofs and this block was mostly brownstones.

The gunman looked down, saw me looking up, and snapped off a quick shot. The bullet ripped a hole in the concrete floor of the patio.

I sprinted for the kitchen, shouldering through the

3

cooks and dishwashers who were crowding around the doorway. I told them to stay inside. Then I dialed 911 on the kitchen phone.

A lady cop said, "Police emergency."

I said, "There's a dead man in the patio behind Pal Joey's on West Fiftieth. Tell the officers to come through the alleyway alongside the club."

The lady had some questions, but I hung up. Telling Angelo Sampietro, our fat chef, to keep the kitchen help indoors, I went back into the dining salon. This was the main room of the club, legal capacity 250 persons, but it was Saint Patrick's Day, so we had a few more. From any point in the salon you could see all the tables and the bar. The southern and eastern walls were mirrored solid with pier glass.

If the shots had been heard in here, nobody seemed to have noticed. In New York City people don't pay attention to such sounds. I saw many regular customers, friends, and of course a lot of parties from out of town. I looked everyone over, not sure why. There were a few heavies in the room, but there always were, so I don't know what I expected to see by merely looking. I saw the tiny Garay twins, Licia and Lucio, at a table with "Candy the Dandy" Valentino, their impresario. They did Latin American dances. Hymie "Doubles" Gross, the bookie, had a table with Chico Grande, his current contender for the welterweight title, and a pair of show girls. Ruby Porcelain, the Broadway producer, was at another table with Honey Wing, his new blonde. Father Vito Caracciola of Actor's Chapel was at a table with two young actors, handsome Hub Grindel and Mady Prevatte. And so on.

I told Dom Ambrosini, our maitre d', that Jock had been killed, the body was in the patio, and the cops would be

4

along any minute now. He didn't waste time asking questions but quickly alerted the waiters, who in turn informed certain guests, who then handed their guns under the tables to their lady friends for safekeeping in case of a frisk.

I spoke to the head barman, old Jimmy Joyce, who reached under the bar and pressed the little button that flashed red lights in the gaming rooms upstairs on the parlor floor. There were a dozen big spenders up there, city dads and other pillars of society. That room would be empty in two minutes. A stairway led straight to the street.

I went to the front door to wait for the cops and try to steer them around by the alleyway, because I didn't want them stomping through my dining room and upsetting the guests. Jock's young cousin Marco Lucarelli was our doorman. I told him about Jock, and he started to go back. I put a hand on his arm.

"Nothing you can do," I told him. "I need you here."

I threw away my cigar and unwrapped a fresh one. My hands were shaking so hard I couldn't hold the lighter steady. Marco lit it for me.

He asked what happened. I took him outside, on the street, and told him what I'd seen from the window of the john.

"Think Maginnis set him up?"

"It looked that way," I said. "I think maybe he was trying to set me up too. But there could be another explanation."

"Like what?"

"Why would Maginnis kill the goose that laid the golden eggs? He was doing very well with Jock alive."

Marco had more questions, but squad cars were already

5

whooping maniacally all over Times Square and shrieking into both ends of our block. Sidewalk types in front of McAnn's bar down the street scattered like startled pigeons. The cars pulled up in front of the club, red lights flashing, doors flying open, cops piling out like Gangbusters. Marco and I blocked the doorway and tried to persuade them to go around by the side alley.

Then along came a cocky little detective with bright brown eyes and a bushy red mustache and craggy eyebrows, and he took over, ignoring Marco and me.

"Some of you go around the back," he told the other cops in a high-pitched brogue as thick as the bogs he came from. "Some of you stay out front here." The feisty little man faced me then and said, "Who're you?"

I told him I was Joseph Streeter, I played piano here, and I was also co-owner.

"Did you make the call?"

"Yes."

He looked up at the neon sign over the entrance. It was a big blue kangaroo wearing a top hat and a monocle and playing a grand piano.

"I've seen that sign a hundred times," he said, "and I always wondered. Why the kangaroo?"

"In Australia the kangaroo is called a joey," I explained. "My name's Joe. The club is built around me and my piano."

The bright brown eyes looked puzzled, the craggy red brows went up.

"You Australian?"

"No, but I've been there."

"I'm Detective Sergeant Al Sweeney. Homicide. Come with me, please, Mr. Streeter. It's out back, I believe?"

I said it was. He led the way through the front entrance, and I followed, along with half a dozen detectives and uniformed cops in single file like Indians on trail. I needn't have worried about my customers. Except for two or three tables, they loved it. At those two or three tables were some of Jock's people, friends of his uncle Rocco Lucarelli. They sat watchful, silent, somber.

As I followed Sergeant Sweeney across the dining room, Dom came up to me and whispered, "Any instructions, Joe? You call Rocco yet?"

"Call him for me," I said.

I continued after Sergeant Sweeney. Near the bar, I felt a sharp rap on my shoulder. I stopped. It was Iovannis "Gentleman John" Volos, a perfumed, heavily bejeweled, hugely fat Greek known as the Patriarch because he ran the rackets down in Chelsea, the Greek numbers, protection to the souvlaki joints and wholesale florists, the Greek cathouses, the hashish traffic, and so forth. He was a frequent guest at Pal Joey's, sometimes for our North Italian cuisine, tonight just at the bar, and he often played cards upstairs. This evening he'd brought Athena Hosnani, a blue-eyed, black-haired, classically beautiful, young and petite but superbly built Egyptian belly dancer. I'd seen them come in together about a half hour earlier, though she was not with him at the moment. Gone to the powder room, no doubt.

Volos asked, "What's happening, Joe?"

I told him Jock had been killed. Gentleman John was a natural actor, always onstage. Now he improvised a whole Greek tragedy. His fat face drooped like a basset hound's, his heavy jowls hung sadly, his double chins despaired.

"I can't tell you how sorry I am," he said hoarsely, his

voice hushed and trembling. "Who could have done such a terrible, terrible thing? Who would want poor Jock dead?"

You, I thought, for one. Volos had made several offers to buy Pal Joey's, and we'd always refused to discuss it. Not that this could be motive for murder. Still, who knew what Gentleman John Volos might consider motive?

I had made reservations for dinner and an early show at one of Volos's clubs, the Eurydice, for the next night. Athena Hosnani danced there, and as a ballerina my Vickie took a professional interest in Athena's work. But now I didn't think Vickie would want to go, what with Jock dead, for she'd been fond of him. So I told Volos to cancel. He expressed regrets and said he understood.

"I thought we would see Vickie here tonight," he said. "Wasn't she coming in on an early flight? Athena had hoped to visit with her this evening."

"She should have been here by now," I said. "But she'll be here or she would have called. Stick around."

Sergeant Sweeney was yelling at me from the kitchen door, "Come on, Streeter! You can tell your customers about it later."

I excused myself to Volos, asked him to give my regards to Athena, and hurried after the sergeant. I followed him and his men through the kitchen and into the patio. More detectives and uniformed cops, who'd gone through the alleyway, were already there. Sweeney sent some of them over the patio walls to see what was on the other side. He also sent a couple of detectives up the fire escape. I watched them, wondering what they'd find up there. A wind was blowing from the west, tossing the leafless tree-tops.

The forensics people had arrived and started making

photographs of the body and measuring the height of the walls and the length and width of the patio, searching the ground for ejected shells, taking blood samples from the brain-spattered wall. They found the shell right away. Caliber 9 mm, known as a "Luger round."

Sergeant Sweeney got out a small notebook and a ballpoint pen.

"Now," he said. "Tell me all about it, Streeter." He was not looking at me but around the patio, taking note of the position of the body, the height of the walls (nine feet), the iron-gated entrance to the alleyway (still open), the cellar doors (padlocked), the patio furniture. I waited for him to ask specific questions. He told the police photographer, "I want long shots and close-ups from every angle, and I want you to go up the fire escape and take an overhead shot. Shoot whatever else you want to, but give me what I said." The photographer looked like he could bite nails. Sweeney saw it and said, "Sure you got film in that camera?" The photographer's face reddened. He looked as Irish as the sergeant. But he said nothing. Sweeney then turned to me. "You said you made the call?"

"Yes."

"Who's the dead man?"

"Giacomo Alfieri, my partner."

"Would you spell that, please?"

I did so. He wrote it down. Then he looked up at me. *"That's* Jock Alfieri?"

"Did you know him?" I asked.

"Only by sight," he said. He bent down to look more closely at Jock's face. The bullet had entered just above the left eye, making a small red hole. When it came out it carried away the top of his head. "Happened just now, did it?"

9

"Yes."

"Anybody else hear the shot?"

"The whole neighborhood, I should think."

"That's how you knew about it? You heard the shot?"

"I saw it happen. I was in the employees' rest room. I looked out the window, and I could see Jock, right where you're standing. His back was to the window. The killer came up behind him, from the right. I saw the gun and yelled to Jock to look out. He turned toward me and got it in the face."

"The window was open, the way it is now?"

"Yes."

Sweeney was writing everything down in his little notebook.

"Did you recognize the killer?"

"No."

"Jock Alfieri was your partner in this club, you said. Were you equal partners? I mean, did you own equal shares?" I said yes. Apparently the cocky little man was fishing for motive. "Besides being business partners, were you friends?"

"Buddies," I said. "Both bachelors."

"Excuse me," Sweeney said. He quickly patted me down. "Sorry," he said. "You understand how it is." I said I did. He said, "What's on the other side of these walls?"

"Back yards," I said. "The Actor's Chapel abuts this one."

"You or your late partner know the people in this block?"

"Some of them—street characters, merchants, musicians who hang out at McAnn's bar . . ."

"Who works here at the Pal Joey's? I mean, the regulars —the chef, the headwaiter . . ."

"The chef is Angelo Sampietro, the maitre d' is Dom Ambrosini, the head barman Jimmy Joyce, doorman Marco Lucarelli . . ."

I spelled out the names for him. He wrote them down.

"Lucarelli," he said. "Name's familiar." He studied my face as if waiting for me to help him out. I didn't. "It'll come to me," he said. "Can you describe the man who shot your partner?"

I said the gunman was short, slender, had a black rat's-tail mustache, a small goatee, long sideburns, dressed very sharp, wore large pink sunglasses.

Sweeney stopped writing and looked around the garden again.

"Any idea why your partner was out here this time of the night?" I said no. "Well, why *would* he come out here at midnight? The patio don't look like it's open for business."

"Maybe he came out for a breath of air," I said.

"In this city?" Sweeney looked up at me from under the craggy red eyebrows with a suspicious glint in his eyes. "All right, now, Streeter. Tell me, if you can, why was Alfieri facing *that* way?"

"I don't understand."

"Well, you said he was facing away from you, when you called to him to warn him about the gunman, right?"

"That's right."

"So he must have been facing the alley gate. How come?"

"How come he was facing the alleyway?"

Sweeney nodded, smiling expectantly. I gave it very little thought, because at this point Detective Lieutenant Michael Maginnis came striding into the patio from the alley. He walked straight up to Sweeney and me and

11

greeted us both by our first names.

"What's happening?" he said. "I was just passing by. My night off." He looked down at Jock. "Dear God!" he said. "Who did it?"

"You knew him?" Sweeney asked.

"A little," Maginnis said. "I come here for dinner sometimes. Ever hear Streeter play the piano, Al? Plays fine piano, this boy. Real old good-time jazz. Worth the price of admission."

Maginnis was grinning at me. One of my many admirers. So I couldn't rat on a friend of mine, could I? Also I was thinking about the gaming rooms upstairs, empty now. And there were other thoughts to think, but that one was enough.

So I didn't answer Sergeant Sweeney's question: Jock had been facing the alleyway because he'd been facing Lieutenant Maginnis, and here was the big mick himself, bold as brass. His tiny pig eyes were fixed on mine, and I wondered what he'd do if I told Sergeant Sweeney what I knew. I had a hunch I wouldn't get very far into my story. I was remembering a case in the Marines before War Two when a supply sergeant gunned down a merchant he'd been cheating with. He'd also been cheating the merchant. They were having a conference in the middle of the parade ground, where they couldn't be overheard, but the battalion commander, who was a suspicious type, came along just then, so the supply sergeant shot the merchant dead, right in front of the colonel, then bent over the dead man, came up with a switchblade, and swore he'd saved his dear colonel's life. He had to stand a general court-martial, but he beat it. Of course, that was in Honduras, and the merchant was a bandido anyway.

One of the men Sergeant Sweeney had sent up the fire

escape came down now and reported.

"The fire escape's dusty," he said. "We found some partial footprints, enough to make a composite. Looks like somebody wearing small shoes with pointy toes and little heels."

Sergeant Sweeney said, "How about that, Streeter? Still say you saw a man go up the fire escape? Not a woman dressed like a man?"

"He had a mustache and a goatee," I said.

The man who was making the report said, "Sergeant, we also found this."

He offered Sweeney what looked like a rat's tail. Sweeney took it between his thumb and forefinger. He stared at it as if it really were a rat's tail.

"May I see it?" I said. He dangled it to me. I took it, held it to my nose, and sniffed it. "Gum arabic," I told him. "Actor's glue." I examined the underside. "Here, Sergeant, you can see traces of glue on the false hair."

He looked and said, "You could be a detective, Streeter." I'm sure he meant it kindly. "You still say the killer was a man?" I shrugged. "How come you know about this stuff, this actor's glue, and false hair? You ever been an actor?"

"No, just a piano player. But I've worked with actors in clubs here and there."

"Where you from, Streeter?"

"San Francisco."

"That where you learned to play the piano?"

"Where I started."

"What did you do before that?"

"Played in the sandbox with the little girl next door."

He laughed like a good straight man. Then he fed me another line.

"So you always been a piano player?"

I decided not to take advantage of him and just said yes, I'd picked it up by ear when I was a child and I'd been playing all over the world since I first hit the street at the age of twelve.

"How does a piano player acquire co-ownership of a club like this?"

Of course, he wasn't the first to pop that question, so I had a stock answer: "Plain living and high thinking."

Sergeant Sweeney looked like I'd just slapped his face. I don't know which I love less, merchants or cops.

Maginnis felt motivated to mix in and said, "The sergeant knows all the questions, Joe. He's our number-one rat-catcher. Sergeant Aloysius Sweeney, terror of the underworld."

I said I had to get back inside and entertain the people. They'd paid to hear me, and they were entitled. So if there was nothing else . . .

"One or two small points is all," Sergeant Sweeney said. "You gave us a fine description of the killer, and now we can't use it. Phony mustache, probably a phony beard, phony sideburns. So who knows what he really looks like. Or *she*. Could the killer be an actor, you think?"

"Lots of people know about false hair and gum arabic," I said. "You can even buy ready-made mustaches and sideburns."

"Think you'd recognize the face without the false hair?"

"And big pink sunglasses, Sergeant."

"Did the killer see *you*?"

"Had to," I said. "He'd heard me yell at Jock to look out. After he shot Jock he turned toward the rest room win-

14

dow. I ducked, but he saw me."

"What kind of gun?"

I thought I'd seen a Walther Parabellum 9 mm, the well-known P-38. Since I owned one myself, I felt an urge not to identify the killer's piece. Sergeant Aloysius Sweeney was sooner or later going to toss the whole building, especially my apartment, in the normal course of his homicide investigation, and he'd find my gun in the drawer of the nightstand by my bed. Still, I felt reluctant to identify the killer's gun. What I was thinking was highly paranoid, but even paranoids have enemies.

I said, "It was a handgun, Sergeant. I didn't get a really good look. Don't know that much about guns anyway."

"Could you tell if it was a revolver or an automatic?"

"Automatic, I think."

He put away his ballpoint and notebook and asked if I wanted police protection. I said no. He thought about that, looking up at me with inquisitorial eyes. I wondered how much he knew about Pal Joey's operation.

"Well, it's up to you," he said. "I can't make you accept a bodyguard if you won't have one. But this club is a public place, and I'm going to put some men here, in front, in back, inside. Don't worry; they'll be in plain clothes. They won't disturb your customers."

"If you insist," I said.

"I do," Sweeney said. "Now, we know the killer went up the fire escape. I wonder why. He could have run out through the alley. Was the alley gate locked? It isn't now. Don't you keep it locked? Easy access from the street."

"We do keep it locked," I said. "I didn't notice if it was locked when I came out. Perhaps it wasn't. But I did see the killer going up the fire escape. I would have gone after him, but he was already at the third floor."

"Good thing you didn't," Sweeney said. "He could have shot you like a pigeon."

"He tried," I said. I pointed to the hole the killer's 9 mm slug had gouged in the concrete floor. "I flew through the kitchen doorway."

"Smart pigeon," said Sweeney. "Still and all, I wonder why he went up the fire escape when he might have run out through the alley more easily. What do you think, Streeter?"

Well, I thought maybe the killer was afraid Maginnis would be waiting for him in the alleyway, but here was himself watching me, tense and ready. So I told Sergeant Sweeney that I hadn't the foggiest notion why the killer left by the fire escape instead of the alley. And I reminded him that I was overdue at the piano.

Maginnis took a deep breath, his belly swelled, he smiled at me like an Irish wolfhound.

"What's upstairs?" Sergeant Sweeney asked. "How many apartments?"

"Only one," I said. "The parlor floor is banquet rooms with a separate kitchen and service bar. The third floor is a photography studio. And the top floor is my apartment."

The sergeant whipped out his ballpoint and notebook again.

"You said you're a bachelor?"

"I am."

"How come you need a whole floor?"

"Front parlor, bedroom, guest bedroom, dining room, and music room," I said. "Why not? I make a lot of money, Sergeant."

"What about Alfieri?"

"What about him?"

16

"Where did he live?"

"Jersey."

"Where in Jersey?"

"Short Hills."

Sweeney wrote it down. Short Hills is one of those New Jersey communities, like Bay Ridge in Brooklyn or Lido Beach on Long Island, that have certain prosperous Italian families in their midst and are therefore peaceful communities. No muggings, no unauthorized murders. Jock's uncle Rocco Lucarelli had businesses in Newark and New York City, but he spent most of his time in Newark, and he lived in nearby Short Hills. And as Jock's father was dead, he and his mother lived with her brother Rocco and his family in the enormous Lucarelli mansion. These were details that Sweeney would eventually dig up on his own. I did not do his work for him.

"Did Alfieri commute every day?"

"Yes."

"Drive his own car?"

Jock always parked in the lot across from Polyclinic Hospital, a block west of the club. A 1975 Continental with Jersey plates. I had keys because I often borrowed it. There was a snub-nose Miroku .38 in the glove compartment. No license.

I said, "He usually took the bus, sometimes the train."

Sergeant Sweeney finished jotting down his notes and put away the pad and ballpoint again.

"Could the killer get into the building from the fire escape? I can't think why he'd do that, but could he?"

"He'd need a set of keys," I said. "The windows all have gates, and the hall doors are double-locked with dead-bolt locks and police locks."

"What about the keys, then? Can you account for them?

17

I take it there's more than one set in a big place like this."

"There are only three complete sets," I said. "I have one, Jock had one, and there's a spare set in the office safe. There are several partial sets, of course, for the chef, the maitre d', and the head barman. Those sets don't have keys to the doors on the fire escape landings."

The morgue wagon attendants and an assistant medical examiner were about to remove Jock's body. Suddenly I really began to feel the loss, like a flesh wound that takes a while to start hurting. Jock had been more than a partner to me. We were good friends. On nights off we often hung out together. In the joints around Times Square we were known as Mutt and Jeff because he was short and I'm a little taller than average. He was only five-seven and I'm six-one. We'd pick up a pair of broads and bring them back to my place and party all night sometimes. We were pretty tight. I felt my throat choking up, my heart was pounding, I wanted to cry. I cursed. A few tears escaped. I took out my handkerchief and wiped them away.

Sergeant Sweeney pretended not to notice. He asked one of the detectives what they'd found in the decedent's pockets. The detective read off a list of the contents: wallet, keys, money, nothing unusual. Sweeney took the keys and asked me to identify them. I identified those belonging to the club and the upper floors, including my apartment. I explained to Sergeant Sweeney that Jock occasionally used my place. His wallet contained the usual things: credit cards, driver's license (New Jersey), business and personal cards, and about three hundred dollars in cash. It also contained a photograph of a female nude. Or a nude female. I knew her. But I hadn't known that she'd ever posed in the nude for a photograph.

I figured if Iovannis "Gentleman John" Volos knew about that photo it could be motive for murder, for the naked lady was Athena Hosnani, the Alexandrian belly dancer, and she was Volos's favorite of all the exotic dancers in his several nightclubs.

My late partner's hobby, his avocation, was photography, though not exclusively nudes. He shot landscapes, seascapes, portraits, still lifes, and abstractions, in black-and-white or color, still or movie.

Sergeant Sweeney admired Athena Hosnani's nude photo for a long, contemplative moment, and said, "Know her, Streeter?"

"Can't say I do, Sergeant. I didn't know old Jock went in for porn."

"That isn't pornography," said Sweeney. "That's art!"

"Yeah?" I said. "Okay. Great broad. Lovely tush."

He looked disgusted with me, then looked away, up at the fire escape.

I looked at Maginnis and saw he'd recognized the woman in the photo. But he wasn't saying anything.

Sweeney said, "All right, let's check the hall doors on the fire escape landings." He started for the ladder, turned, and said, "Aren't you coming, Streeter?"

I said no, I really had to get back to work, it was very late and getting later, and people had paid a stiff cover to hear me tickle the ivories.

"Your partner's just been murdered," Sweeney said. "In the circumstances, I don't understand how you can go back in there and play the piano for a bunch of drunks."

I said I was an entertainer and the show must go on. Maybe I'd play some blues. He looked even more disgusted with me. I said my guests weren't a bunch of drunks. We didn't allow drunkenness at Pal Joey's. If a guest couldn't get high without getting drunk he got ejected from the premises.

"Just keep yourself available," Sweeney said. "Don't go anywheres without seeing me first, right?"

He started up the ladder. Figuring he'd probably go through my apartment when he finished with the parlor floor and Jock's photo studio, I called up to him.

"Sergeant!" He stopped on the first landing and looked down. "Be careful," I told him. "I have a dog. She's friendly, but she might growl a little, since you're a stranger. Her name's Heidi. Be gentle and she'll be all right. I call her Heidi or Schatzi. She answers to both names."

"What kind of dog?" Sweeney asked.

"German shepherd."

The morgue men were taking Jock's body away. Now Lieutenant Michael Maginnis and I were alone. Well, not quite. There were still some forensics men pottering about.

Maginnis said, "Where can we talk?"

"In the alley," I said. "You go first."

I followed him. I don't carry a gun when I'm working or I might have shot him then and there in the alleyway. As it was, I itched to lay hands on him. We were about the same size and build, six-one and one-ninety, and the same age, no longer in the first blush of youth. I look older because my hair is white, but it's been snow white since I was forty and caught a tropical fever in Brazil. I'm in shape, however, and I could have killed Maginnis with my bare hands. Pianists have very strong fingers. I could have crushed his windpipe faster than it takes to tell it. Unless, of course, he shot me first.

He stopped halfway along the narrow alley. There were

cops coming and going, but they kept moving. We could speak freely. It was dark here and damp from an early-evening shower. It smelled of stale urine. Street characters used it as a public pissoir. Though a brisk breeze was whipping along Fiftieth Street, the air in the alleyway was still. Dank as a tomb.

"I know what it looked like," Maginnis said. "But it wasn't that way. Believe me."

"You ran."

"For Christ's sake, what was I supposed to do—stand there and get shot?"

"You had time to crank off a round. Jock was in the line of fire, so the hitter had to take him before he could get you. You had time enough. But you ran."

"I didn't happen to have my piece with me—"

"Come *off* it! Since when does a cop go without his gun?"

"I just never wore it when I was coming to see Jock. I know the regulation, Joe, but lots of cops—"

"Bullshit, Maginnis! What happened on your paydays around here? You're telling me you'd pick up your money and walk unarmed? With a thousand dollars in your pocket? In this mugalopolis? Don't insult my intelligence."

"Well, I felt I had friendly relations with Jock, you know, and guns—"

"Shove it! Tell it to the Marines. Tell it to your mother. 'Friendly relations'! Your 'friendly relations' were pretty goddamned expensive at a thousand clams a month. Some friendship! But I've got news for you, baby. Your friendship isn't worth dog shit now. So bugger off. Scat."

"Joe, listen! You're being unfair. You can't hang this on me. I didn't know nothing about it, I swear on my

21

mother's grave. I just come to talk business with Jock. Didn't he tell you?"

I remembered. Jock had in fact mentioned something about Maginnis wanting to see him tonight. We'd been down in the office during the afternoon, going through an old routine with our lawyer-accountant, Charlie Green, who thought I should take more of an interest in the business end of Pal Joey's. He couldn't understand my lack of interest. I'd never explained to him that I hated business. Charlie Green loved it. But then, Charlie was a freak. So unless I was willing to tell him I considered business worthy only of thieves, I had to go through this ritual from time to time. Trying to get me interested in business, he was like a Jewish mama trying to get her kid to take castor oil. Just one spoonful, darling, and you can have some chicken soup. With *lukshen.* Anyway, during the nonsense with Charlie Green there'd been this call from Maginnis saying he was coming to the club along toward midnight and he wanted to see both of us, Jock and me. Right. I'd forgotten that part too: both of us.

"He did mention it," I told Maginnis. "Must have slipped my mind."

My rusty old brain was beginning to turn its wheels. I could hear them creaking a ragged E flat on a rusty string. The wheels creaked and the wires twanged, but the brain was working at last. Maginnis without his gun? In a pig's eye! He was wearing it now. I saw the bulge on his right hip. He was lying, of course. He'd set up his own mother for a price. And call it business.

That was the name of the game. Business. But who was running it? Not Lieutenant Michael Maginnis. I didn't think he could run a game of tiddlywinks.

"So you see?" he said.

22

"Yeah," I said. "I see, Mike."

"Then you'll keep me out of this?"

"Like I've been doing," I said.

"Right. And thanks, Joe."

"Only one thing, Mike. You were asking Jock for more money. You'll have to forget that now."

"Sure. I understand."

"You're a real sport," I said.

"You're a prince, Joe."

"You too, Mike."

We shook hands firmly and left each other.

❧ 2 ❧

I WENT BACK into the club. It was one o'clock and the people were growing impatient. I opened with Jock's favorite, my pianistic version of Alphonse Picou's great riff from "High Society." It's best on clarinet, but one does what one can. Mady Prevatte came up and sang the chorus, took a bow, and went back to her table with Hub Grindel and Father Vito. She could have had a career as a jazz singer, but she wanted to be an actress. She looked like a young Mae West, and who needs two Mae Wests in one century? So once in a while she'd come up and do a number with me. Pal Joey's had originally been a kind of café theater where professional artists could show their stuff. A showcase. If you didn't have a gig and you wanted to be seen and heard, you could sit in with me. Earlier that evening the Garay twins, Licia and Lucio, had danced for the people. They had a nice act. They were both about five feet tall, they both wore white tie and tails, and they were very cute. Tonight they'd done their bit called the

"Kama Sutra Tango," with me playing the old Argentine number "Adiós Muchachos." They were very athletic and managed to assume several Kama Sutra positions while dancing. I used to have a dozen different acts every night when I owned Pal Joey's alone. But after Jock Alfieri bought in, and the gaming rooms opened on the parlor floor, the price of admission went up and the economics of Pal Joey's changed. The cover was five dollars. Booze was two-fifty a shot. So musicians and singers and other entertainers who used to drop in when there was no cover, no minimum, and the price of a slow beer was fifty cents, naturally didn't drop in anymore. And it wasn't just the price that kept them out. It was also the audience. Well, of course they go together. Your best audience is not the filthy rich; it's your fellow artists. And the price was too high for them. These were matters I had put out of my mind and kept out for some time now, but with Jock dead it was all coming back. Maybe I could get the operation back on its original café theater basis.

Athena Hosnani had come back from the powder room, or wherever she'd gone, and was sitting again by Gentleman John Volos at the bar. They were watching me and smiling, and she was tapping her foot to the beat. I followed "High Society" with "Hava Nagila" and she all but did a belly dance on her bar stool. She was very high, probably on Volos's hashish. That face! A lot of it was theatrical makeup, of course, but still . . . Her flesh was very white, her eyes large and a clear, cold sapphire blue. She had fine lines, nose thin and straight, chin firm and delicately rounded, mouth generous and full, lips parted now in a brilliant smile. She had glossy black hair, which she wore braided in a coronet, and I knew it was truly black and not a dye job because I'd seen that nude photo

25

in Jock's wallet. Collar and cuffs matched, all right. I gave "Hava Nagila" a lot of left hand, getting to her, and I could tell she wanted to come up and dance, but with Volos there I knew she wouldn't. She had once, one night when she'd come in without him, but never again. Apparently he didn't want her shaking it anywhere but in his own club, the Eurydice.

I saw Hub Grindel giving me the office, which meant he wanted to join me and do his turn. He was a good-looking young actor without much talent, destined for Hollywood, not New York, but he had a rather funny bit that he did. It wasn't much, but it always brought down the house. Someone must have told him that brevity is the soul of wit, because his act was very brief. He did one-liners, but only one. He'd get up, do one, take a quick bow, and sit down. So when I finished "Hava Nagila" he came up. I waited, letting him have it all to himself.

He approached the microphone slowly, leaned into it, and said, completely deadpan, "Humpty Dumpty—was pushed. . . ." He waited, looking at the floor. It caught on like a fragmentation grenade: you pull the pin, and wait. When the laugh came, he took his quick bow and went back to his table. I played "Post Time." No, it wasn't in bad taste, for he didn't know about Jock. And even if he had, we were entertainers, weren't we? Besides, it was true: Humpty Dumpty was pushed.

Sergeant Sweeney stood by the kitchen door, watching. He looked very unhappy. He waited until I'd finished playing my last number, a blues medley: "Tin Roof," "Yaller Dog," "C-Jam," and the "Bye-Bye Blues." I stood up to take the bow, and Sweeney beckoned to me, but the people wanted an encore, so I gave them another shot of the Picou riff from "High Society." That always gets them.

You could be Jelly Roll Morton or just plain Joe Streeter, no matter: that riff leaves them happy.

I closed the piano and went to Sweeney and took him to my private table in a back corner. He refused a drink, accepted coffee.

While we waited for his coffee and my usual cognac, he said, "I enjoyed the music, Streeter." I didn't think so. He looked glum. He said, "I'd like to hear some more sometime."

"No time like now," I said. "What's your pleasure?"

"I have bad news for you," he said. "It's your dog. She's dead. Somebody shot her."

What Jock's death couldn't do, the murder of Schatzi did very effectively. I started to get up from the table. I was going to see her. Sweeney put a hand on my arm. I couldn't breathe for crying. It was as if something was working my chest like a bellows. And it took a while to stop. Dom saw me and came over. Sweeney shooed him away. I don't think anyone else noticed. My back was to the people. Schatzi was only two years old. Beautiful, loving. She was a silvery shepherd, and she had the most soulful eyes I have ever seen on man, woman, or beast. I walked her three times a day, and everyone in the neighborhood knew her. And loved her.

Sweeney let me grieve awhile, then said, "I found a Walther Parabellum, right?"

"I've got a license," I said.

"Well, maybe that'll help a little," he said. "But the gun's been fired recently. It still smells of gunpowder."

I said, "Maybe it isn't my gun?"

"It was in the drawer of the nightstand by your bed, Streeter. So let's have a look at the license."

"It's in the safe," I said, "down in the office."

27

"Good. Let's go."

But his coffee and my cognac came then, so we took our time.

I said, "Sergeant, you don't really believe I killed my partner and my dog, do you? No matter whose gun you found in my bedroom . . ."

"I do not," he said. He loaded his coffee with sugar. "It's an obvious frame. Though you could have done it. We haven't got a corroborating witness. That's bad. There's some who'd take you in for lack of a better suspect." He took a long slurp of coffee. "You say you saw the hit from the employees' rest room window, then came around through the hall and the kitchen to the patio, saw someone going up the fire escape, dodged a bullet, ducked back into the kitchen, and called 911. Right?" I said it was. "Good. Now, purely for the sake of discussion, let's assume you iced your partner, climbed the fire escape to your apartment, snapped off a parting shot at the corpse, just to make sure—and missed, at that range—then let yourself into your apartment, stashed the gun without cleaning it, and came down again the same way. Or maybe you came down by an inside stairway. Was the back door to the kitchen open or closed?"

"Closed."

"So nobody but you saw the shooting. And no one saw *you.*"

"The murderer did."

"As you say, the murderer did."

"Sergeant, why would I stash a murder weapon in my own apartment, a gun licensed in my name, and then call the cops? And who would shoot his own dog?"

"Oh, I agree," said Sweeney. "Only a nut would set up a double frame. Not that it hasn't been tried. You ever

28

been to see a psychiatrist or spent time in a mental institution?" I laughed hollowly. "Still and all," he said, "we did find what looks like the murder weapon in your apartment. So let's go and get that license and just make sure it's your gun, okay?"

"If it is," I said, "then what?"

"Then we'll see."

"What about motive?" I asked. "Jock and I were equal partners. Fifty-fifty down the middle. And with the business we've been doing, that's a lot of bread. I had more than enough; no reason to want his share or any part of it. In fact, I cleared more than he did, because I own my half outright, and he . . ."

I shouldn't have said it. My only excuse is that Jock's murder had blown my cool. I've never been famous for thinking on my feet anyway. I think sitting down, and my fingers do the thinking. But I wasn't about to go on and explain my remark. Jock's backer, his uncle Rocco Lucarelli, was well known as an operator of numerous untaxable enterprises, and over the years his name had appeared on a few police blotters. Nothing heavy, but nothing legal either.

"Well," Sweeney said, "I don't know whether you know this, but we don't have to establish motive. So what were you saying about equal shares in the business? Would you mind developing that a little?"

I said, "I don't really know anything about Jock's end of it. I always kept out of the business. Can't handle arithmetic. When I add two plus two I get a pair of deuces. If you want any business information, talk to Charles H. Green, our accountant. He's also our lawyer."

"Heard of him," Sweeney said. He got out his ballpoint and notebook and wrote it down. "Funny thing," he said.

"We found ten thousand dollars in used tens and twenties in a film pack container in the darkroom of the photography studio upstairs. Know anything about it?"

"No."

"All right," he said. "Let's go see the license for that gun."

As we passed the bar on our way to the cellar stairs, Athena Hosnani spoke to me. She wasn't smiling now.

"Iovannis just told me," she said. Her lower lip trembled, and her eyes were brimming with tears that didn't quite spill over. I wouldn't have thought those cold, clear sapphire eyes could cry. They were the coldest blue I'd ever seen. Volos was doing his Greek tragedy bit, though he'd been smiling earlier. Athena said, "Poor Jock! Who did it?"

I said we didn't know. She asked about Vickie, if she'd got in yet. I said she was overdue, but she'd be here before closing time. She would have called if she weren't coming, I said, but I had the uneasy feeling that I was whistling in the dark. Airplanes are the safest form of travel, according to the airlines companies, who figure their safety statistics in accidents per passenger mile. If they figured by passenger hours they'd scare customers away. I wanted to get to a phone and call Chicago. Vickie lived with two other dancers, and they'd know if she left at all. But in the circumstances I didn't want to call her number on one of our club phones. Things were happening that I didn't understand. Not only Jock's murder. My gun had been fired recently, but not by me. And what was Jock doing with ten grand cash in his darkroom?

Sweeney was standing at my elbow. Athena gave him the sapphire stare. She must have smelled cop. I wondered if he recognized the gorgeous nude in Jock's wallet photo.

Then I noticed that Dom was in the middle of the room trying to catch my eye. I excused myself and went over to him.

He said, "I called Rocco from outside. He wants to see you. He says you should take a hotel for the night. He'll see you at the hotel. That's what he says. So which hotel?"

I thought about it. Uncle Rocco wouldn't want me leading a gang of cops to him, and I felt pretty sure Sergeant Sweeney was going to put me under surveillance. He'd put a tail on me when I left the club, but if you know your Manhattan you can easily shake the smartest tail, unless of course he doesn't care if you know he's tailing you.

"Try the Plaza," I told Dom.

He said, "Any idea who shot Jock?"

"None," I said.

"You think it was personal?"

"Business," I said. "Maybe personal too. You any ideas?"

"Marco says Maginnis set him up."

"It looked that way. I'd bet on it, but I can't prove it. I talked with Maginnis. Of course he denies it. But it's Rocco's problem, isn't it?"

Dom straightened, gave me a stiff-backed bow, and said, "I'll take care of the hotel."

"Vickie's supposed to be flying in from Chicago, and she's long overdue," I said. "She ought to be here, or phone, or wire. If she shows after I leave, tell her where I am. I want you to close up tonight."

He gave me the stiff-backed bow again. Sergeant Sweeney came over to us and asked me if we could please get on with the investigation. I led the sergeant toward

31

the door at the back end of the bar and gave Jimmy the signal. The head barman pressed the button under the bar that unlocked the door. Two stairways led from this door, one to the upper floors and one down to the cellar, where we had our office.

I unlocked the cellar door and we went in, four of us, the sergeant and I and two of his detectives. Though a part of the cellar had been partitioned off for storage, the office area was large and comfortable. It had a safe, some filing cabinets, and a roll-top desk for our accountant. It also had a service bar and several big overstuffed leather chairs and coffee tables. Business conferences were held down here when Jock's uncle and his Newark associates conferred with their New York counterparts. I didn't attend these meetings, but sometimes Jock did. And that was a whole can of ravioli I didn't intend to open for the likes of Sergeant Sweeney, though I had no doubt his investigation would eventually get into it.

While I was working the combination to the safe, Sweeney and his men prowled the office, going through Charlie Green's desk, fumbling in the filing cabinets. I opened the safe and took out my gun license in its small manila envelope. I noticed the account books were missing and figured Charlie had probably taken them home to juggle them a little.

"What's the rest of the cellar like?" Sweeney asked.

"Storage space," I told him, "for the kitchens and bars. That's the bathroom over there."

"Did Alfieri shoot the nude photo we found in his wallet?"

The question had been long coming.

"So you searched his studio," I said.

"You didn't tell me the photography studio was your

partner's. How come you didn't mention that, Streeter?"

"Why should I?"

"When I told you we'd found ten grand cash in a film pack in the darkroom, you didn't mention that the studio was Alfieri's. I wonder why." I shrugged it off. "Somebody got there first," he said. "You can see where some pictures were taken off the walls. Not all of them. Some were left. I'm wondering what was taken, what kind of pictures they were, why those and not the others."

I had a hunch. Jock had all kinds of big exhibition prints on those walls, and a lot of them were female nudes. Not porn. Sweeney called it right when he said art. Jock's nude photos were sexy but not crude, not raunchy. They were done with taste, lovely and graceful. I knew some of the people who'd modeled for those nudes. Most were professional models. Many were young actresses. Some were hookers. And a few were women whose faces adorned the society pages of Sunday newspapers. I wondered what those women would look like if I took false hair and gum arabic and glued rat's-tail mustaches under their cute little noses and black goatees on their pretty chins. Nude photos could be worth a lot of money. With or without false hair. And Jock had hidden ten thousand dollars cash in his darkroom.

I said, "Sergeant, why would anybody take the photos off his walls? He gave prints away for the asking. Nobody had to steal them. Maybe it was vandalism?"

"I don't think so," Sweeney said. I could tell by the look on his face, he wasn't buying my ingenuous attitude. He said, "Someone also took all the files from the cabinets in the darkroom. The file drawers are hanging open, empty. The drawers are labeled 'Negatives.' Why would anyone steal the negatives, all of them?"

33

For the same reason the thief took the photos, I was thinking.

"Well, they missed the ten grand," I said brightly.

"I don't think so," Sweeney said. "I don't think they were looking for money. They left some valuable cameras and some other equipment. There's a gadget that looks like it's used for editing motion picture film. That right?"

I said, "I don't know that much about photography, Sergeant."

Well," he said, "if there's film-editing equipment, there should be some movie film, right?"

"There isn't?" I said.

He just looked at me. I worked at unwrapping a fresh cigar. So the still negatives *and* the cans of movie film had been stolen. And certain photos of female nudes. I wondered about Jock's cross-index file, identifying the still photos and the movies. If the cross-index file was there, Sweeney knew it. If not, he wouldn't know it was missing, though he might figure it out eventually. Probably would. The bulldog type.

"So I think we have a robbery-homicide," he said. "Two people, the hitter and the burglar. Now, why would someone kill your partner *and* rob his studio? In the ordinary robbery-homicide, the victim is killed because he resists or witnesses the robbery. Not in this case. Alfieri wasn't in his studio while it was being robbed. He was in the patio getting shot. In other words, the murder wasn't necessary to the robbery. So what's in those missing photographs or in the negatives that could get him killed?"

"I'm afraid I can't help you, Sergeant," I said. "What's left on the walls?"

"Horses, cats, people's faces, waves on a beach, flowers, a ballet dancer, some pictures I couldn't make out."

34

Of course, the photo of the ballet dancer was Victoria Moorcroft, my Vickie. I'd have been worried if that one was missing. And since he hadn't mentioned seeing any female nudes, my hunch was right. That's all that was missing. Nude photos of several women. And since all the negatives had been taken from the file cabinets, either the thief had been in too much of a hurry to sort out the particular ones he or she wanted, or he (she) had taken all of them in order not to single out the ones that could identify him (her) by their absence. For the same reasons the thief would have taken the cross-index file, the whole thing, all the cards. This argued haste. There hadn't been enough time to go through the files of negatives and the cross-index card file. Therefore the murder and the burglary could have happened more or less at the same time. Both *could* have been done by the same person.

I said, "I guess I just never noticed particularly what was on Jock's studio walls, Sergeant. Not the visual type. You know how it is with musicians. We're auditory." I didn't think he'd go for that kind of razzle-dazzle. From the look in his eye, he didn't. "Anyway," I said, "I found my gun license. Here it is."

I handed it to him, and he compared the serial number with a number he had in his little notebook. Then he put the license back in its manila envelope and gave it to one of his men.

"Same gun," he said. "What do you think of a robbery to conceal the motive for homicide? Any ideas?"

"None," I said. "I can't imagine why anyone would want Jock dead. I didn't know he had an enemy."

"Okay, here's where we stand," Sweeney said. "We'll assume ballistics will find that your gun killed Alfieri, so I could take you down on at least suspicion, but your lawyer and accountant, Mr. Charles Green, would spring you as fast as we got you printed. Anyway, I don't believe you iced your partner, shot your own dog, and stole all those negatives and photos. So I'm going along with your story, which means someone got a set of keys, borrowed your gun, shot your dog and your partner, climbed the fire escape, stashed the gun in your apartment, and got away, maybe over the roofs, maybe down the inside stairway and into the club. Can you help me prove it, Streeter?"

"Well, you've got a point there," I said, "about the killer taking the inside stairway. But he wouldn't have to go into the club. He could go straight out to the street."

"So I think we begin with the keys," Sweeney said. "There's three complete sets, you say. You have one. Your partner had one, which I've got. And there's a spare set in the safe?"

"Yes."

"I'd like to see it."

I knelt before the open safe and reached in. The spare set wasn't there. I rummaged around. No good. I stood up.

Sweeney said, "Who knew the combination to the safe?"

"Jock and I and Charlie Green."

"The lawyer-accountant?"

"Yes."

"Nobody else?"

I said nobody, though in fact Jock's uncle knew the combination. I made a quick mental inventory of the safe's contents, as far as I knew them, but then I really wasn't sure what Uncle Rocco or Charlie Green kept in there. What they stashed was no business of mine. I kept only a few legal papers, my Marine Corps discharge, the gun license, and personal stash of cash, and a small cham-

36

ois bag of rough diamonds that I'd picked up in Brazil some years before.

"I keep a personal money reserve in here," I said. "If you don't mind I'll take it now."

Sweeney said he didn't. He watched me as I unlocked one of the little drawers in the safe and took out my bundle of bills. I was able at the same time to palm the small chamois bag of rocks. I slid the whole boodle into my inside coat pocket.

The diamonds were hot. Not exactly stolen, but hot anyway. I had not informed the Brazilian government that I'd found them, and I had not declared them to U.S. Customs when I came up from Brazil. But that's another story, called smuggling. It was also the answer to Sergeant Sweeney's question: "How does a piano player acquire co-ownership in a club like this?" I've played jazz piano all over the world, or most of it: at the Club Eco in Mexico City, the old Jockey Club in Havana before the revolution, the Gung Ho in Hong Kong, the Pink Gin in Sydney, the Club Cachassa in Belém, which is two degrees south of the Equator at the mouth of the Amazon River. I'd been trying for years to get up a grubstake so I could open my own club in New York, and one day I got lucky. A mail plane carrying a shipment of Brazilian rough diamonds to Surinam had crashed. The location was known. The only approach was by boat and then by foot through jungle. There must have been hundreds of scavengers trying to get to that plane, but I owned a surveyed PT boat from War Two and got up the Rio Branco first. From there it was duck soup, piece of cake except for cannibal Indians, homicidal diamond scavengers like myself, and the Brazilian army. But I got away with the rocks.

When I leased and remodeled the old brownstone on

West Fiftieth Street and opened Pal Joey's it wasn't the big, ritzy affair that it became later, but it did very well. It did so well it attracted the attention of Giacomo Alfieri. He hung out at the club, and as he was a good customer and liked jazz, we became friends. When he offered to buy in and upgrade the club it sounded like a good idea. I told him I'd think it over. Then one night he came in with title to the building. I was now leasing it from him. Well, it seemed a little pushy, you might say, but it also demonstrated his seriousness. So he got Charles Horatio Green to draw up some papers, and we were partners in Pal Joey's. He put up half the money for remodeling, reequipping, and so forth. I sold off some more diamonds to get up my half. When we reopened I still had maybe a hundred carats in the little chamois bag.

The business went well from the start. But it was no longer the old Pal Joey's, where musicians and other unemployed entertainers could afford to hang out. And by then I'd found out that Jock had a backer, his uncle Rocco Lucarelli. Lots of people in the entertainment world have reason to be grateful to backers like Uncle Rocco. Trouble, when it came, didn't come from Rocco. It came from his nephew, my partner. But not only from Jock, for it takes two to make trouble. The other party was something wearing a false rat's-tail mustache, or whoever had sent him or her.

"Who knew about your gun?" Sweeney asked.

"I never flashed it," I said. "But it's no secret."

"Well, all we found in your apartment was the gun," he said. "Not the spare set of keys. So whoever took them out of that safe still has them, I'd say, which means he can get back into the building anytime he pleases, if he isn't still around here someplace. I think, Streeter, you'd better have all the locks changed first thing tomorrow. Then you can give me a set and keep one for yourself. Better exclude Charles Green for the moment. Let's keep tight control, right? And don't put a spare set in the safe. And maybe you'd better not sleep here tonight. Go to a hotel."

This fit my plans, so I thanked him for his suggestion and told him I agreed with his reasoning. As a witness, I could be a target.

Which would leave only Lieutenant Maginnis, who was likewise a prime witness. Maybe the killer would go for him too. Just an idle thought, but it cheered me.

Sweeney caught me smiling and asked why. I threw him a herring.

"Well, if the killer does come after me," I said, "he'll have to get himself another gun."

"That's funny?" said Sweeney.

"Yeah. And I'll install those locks first thing in the morning like you said."

"I'll have a couple of my men help you."

"No," I said. "Thanks anyway. I'll take care of it. I'm pretty handy, and I like to do things. I've installed all kinds of locks in my time—dead locks, chain locks, Fox locks. . . ."

Sergeant Sweeney gave me a long, hard look, frowning. He wasn't going to ask me if I didn't trust cops to install my locks. But if he had, I would have explained to him why the Fox lock is known as a police lock: It's to keep the police out.

⳧ 3 ⳩

WE HAD CLOSED the kitchen at one o'clock. I played my last set at two. We shut down the bar at three as usual. By four everyone but the help would be gone. It was now three-thirty. Sergeant Sweeney and a few of his men were still prowling. The forensics people had finished and packed up their gear. And still I had not heard from Vickie.

I told Sweeney I was leaving. He asked which hotel. I said the Hotel Commodore. It closed down a few weeks later, but on Saint Patrick's Day 1976 it was still open for business. It was a good hotel in its time. Many years ago I played piano in the dining room of the old Commodore. The city should have declared it a landmark.

"I'll have one of our cars take you," Sweeney said.

"Don't bother. I'll grab a cab."

"No," he said. "I insist. You could get lost in this big city."

"You mean I'd skip? What for?"

"Maybe the same reason you told me your partner commuted by train or bus. There's a set of car keys on his key ring."

"Sometimes he drove," I said. "Sometimes he rode the train. What could I tell you?"

"So you're going to your hotel with an escort."

"I thought we agreed there'd be no police bodyguard."

"Just for tonight, Streeter. I could take you into protective custody, of course."

"I'll go quietly," I said. "Tell your men to bring a car around front."

"Where the hell do you think they are?"

"And make it an unmarked car, Sergeant. A blue-and-white could give me a bad name in the neighborhood."

I knew he'd make sure I checked into the Commodore and he'd have someone in the lobby. Had I been a homicide detective, I thought that was the way I'd play it.

On the way out I spoke again to Dom and asked him if he'd been able to get me into the Plaza.

"You're checked in," he said. "I sent Marco. He signed for you and paid. Here's your room key. You're Harold Williams."

I took the key and told him to inform the crew that we were closing down for a couple of weeks out of respect to Jock. Everyone would work on cleaning up until the funeral, then we'd all take a paid vacation until the first of the month. I left him to close up shop.

When I said good night to Marco at the door, he said he was going to kill Lieutenant Maginnis. I told him that it was Rocco's problem.

"Jock was my cousin," he pointed out.

"And Rocco's your father," I reminded him. "Wait for him to tell you. He may want to question Maginnis himself before he decides."

"You questioned him, and what did it get you?"

"I wasn't able to really put it to him," I said. "Too many cops running around. But *you* lay off, Marco. Go on home now. Dom's closing up."

Sergeant Sweeney hadn't heeded my request for an unmarked car. He had a blue-and-white for me. Fiftieth Street was deserted at this hour except for some of our guests on their way out. The street characters who hang out in front of McAnn's bar were gone now, and McAnn's was dark. It was a windy night and chilly. The breeze was blowing from the river, funneling along Fiftieth Street.

The morgue wagon was still there, and attendants were loading Schatzi into it, carrying her on a stretcher as if she were a person, covered by a blanket. Like Jock, she'd be held for examination, for ballistics, for whatever evidence might bear on the murder. I stepped over to the stretcher and pulled back the blanket. She'd been shot between the eyes. Her eyes were open, still beautiful, still loving, trustful. Who, I wondered, would I have to kill for this?

As the blue-and-white carried me down Broadway and over Forty-second Street, a few hookers and hustlers were still on patrol, shivering in the chill wind or huddling in the doorways of cheap hotels. The graveyard shift.

When I got out at the Commodore an unmarked police car was already parked across the street. It had the usual small, discreet radio antenna on the top and the usual pair of thick-necked detectives in the front seat. They worked at not watching me.

There were still a lot of Saint Patrick's Day out-of-town-ers and local drunks commemorating the bicentennial year, for many bars had not yet closed. I went straight to the registration desk. I knew one of the night clerks, old Matt Griffin. He'd been a trumpet player when he was young, but had long since given up the career for steady work in the hotel business. But he could still blow.

Matt was old enough to be my father, and we looked enough alike to be family: same white hair, same black eyes, same frame, though age had thinned his. He sometimes brought his trumpet to my apartment for after-hours jam sessions and now and then on his days off he'd get a wedding or a bar mitzvah if someone needed a trumpeter.

"I heard it on the radio," he said. "Terrible thing. Know who did it?"

I said, "No. The homicide cops are still at the club. They're all over the building. I need a room."

"Single or double?" he asked.

"Single," I said. "Just for tonight."

"Twenty dollars okay?"

I took out the roll and peeled off a twenty and gave it to him.

"I'll have to register," I told him. "There's a car across the street with a couple of detectives in it. Sergeant Sweeney of Homicide is expecting me to sign in here. He may check it later. So we go by the numbers. Sorry. Keep the twenty for yourself anyway."

"If you have to register it's got to be thirty bucks," he said. I gave it to him and he shoved the register at me. "You a suspect?"

"As of right now," I said, "I'm Sergeant Sweeney's only suspect."

I signed my right name: Joseph A. Streeter, 250 West 50th Street, N.Y.C. Matt handed me the key.

"No luggage, right?" he said. "You don't need a bellhop unless you want something? Bottle? Girl?"

"I need a topcoat and hat," I said. "Got anything that'd fit me?"

"Plain or fancy? I got a nice single-breasted chesterfield, banker's gray, and a homburg to match. The coat should fit. What size hat?"

"Seven and three-eighths."

"I'll check it out. Hundred all right? They belonged to a rich guy who died last week. Need anything else? Shoes? Suitcase?"

I gave him the hundred and told him to bring the things to my room himself and try not to let any possible cops in the lobby see him. I went to the elevators and rode up to the eleventh floor. Matt had given me the key to 1115. I found the room, went in, hung my jacket on a chair, and went into the bathroom. I washed my hands and face, dried off, and hung up the towel.

There was a knock on the door. I opened it on the chain, saw Matt, and let him in. The threads were well worth a hundred, probably cost at least three yards new. And the hat fit.

I said, "How's the back stairway?"

"Nobody uses it," he said. "Anything else I can do? Need a gun?"

I said no. I asked him to check the hallway. He opened the door and looked out.

"All clear," he said.

I gave him the room key and said good night. The back stairway led down to a side lobby, and from there you could catch a cab on the Park Avenue ramp, or you could go down another flight and enter Grand Central Station. From Grand Central you can take any one of several

44

trains out of the city. You can also take the East Side IRT subway uptown or downtown or the underground shuttle to Times Square. I took an underground route all the way, first the shuttle one stop to Times Square and then the BMT subway to the Central Park South entrance of the Hotel Plaza.

The main entrance to the lobby is on the plaza itself, but the side entrance is only about a hundred feet from the BMT subway exit. As I came to the top of the subway stairs I looked around carefully before crossing that hundred-foot stretch of open sidewalk. Central Park's treetops were tossing in the wind. It wasn't Jock's assassin who worried me. It was cops. Two big, beefy types in short black topcoats and snap-brim hats were standing across the street by the park. They seemed to be watching the lobby entrance. When they saw me standing at the top of the subway stairs their heads swiveled and fixed on me. They stood with their hands in their coat pockets, staring at me. There was a black '75 Eldorado with New Jersey plates parked by them. NYPD detectives don't usually drive Cadillacs, at any rate not on the job. I walked to the lobby entrance and went in. Same scene as the Hotel Commodore, out-of-towners performing the annual rites of Saint Patrick, drunk but somewhat better dressed than Commodore people, more tuxedos, fur coats, jewels.

I had my key, room 712, so I went straight up. I stopped outside 712 and pressed my ear to the door. I heard two men inside speaking Italian. My key opened the door, but only as far as the chain allowed.

Without putting his face to the opening, a man said, "Who is it?"

I said, "Harold Williams."

"Who?" he said. He looked carefully around the edge

45

of the door. "Oh, yeah," he said. "Right." It was Big Augie Benedetto. As he unlatched the door he said, "It's Joe."

He swung the door open. Uncle Rocco was standing like an old gorilla on the far side of the room, facing the doorway. You could smell the Scotch through the cigar smoke. Good Scotch. Havana cigars. There was also a bottle of cognac, since Rocco knew my taste. He gave me a gorilla hug as if he'd been not only Jock's uncle but mine too. He looked worried.

"They tail you here?" he asked.

I said, "Not unless those two boys downstairs by the black '75 Eldorado with Jersey plates are cops."

He laughed and said, "How are you, Joey? Take off the coat, sit down, have a drink, tell me what happened."

I took off my coat and hat. Rocco poured me a drink. Big Augie stayed by the door. Augie Benedetto was Uncle Rocco's full-time bodyguard, went everywhere with him, lived at the house in Short Hills, ate with the family, and wore two guns at all times—a Colt .45 automatic under his right arm (he was a lefty) and a pocket Mauser 6.35 mm automatic strapped to his right ankle. Also he didn't drink. Part of the job. A glass or two of red at meals, that's all. Uncle Rocco drank Scotch, lots of it, so he had to have a cold sober bodyguard.

I accepted a panetela. He left the cigar case open on the coffee table between us. He flew his Havanas in from Montreal, a few dozen boxes at a time. Not that the old gorilla had good taste. He simply bought the most expensive of everything—Scotch, tobacco, call girls, cars. The Cadillac is as good as any foreign car. After all, how good can a car get? His wife had one. His son Marco had one. Only Jock was different. His short was a '75 Continental. And as it happened, Rocco asked about it.

"Where did Jock park his car?"

"I don't know," I said. "He usually puts it in the parking lot on the roof of the Port Authority Bus Terminal."

Well, I thought I'd better get Jock's gun out of the glove compartment and see what else there might be. I had a hunch he might have stashed the cross-index file of the photo negatives and movie films in the trunk. There could also be copies of the movies. There had to be copies somewhere. If I sent Rocco to the parking lot across from Polyclinic Hospital, I'd have to get a gun someplace else. You can't be too careful buying an illegal piece, and Jock's little snub-nose Miroku .38 was a good working gun. Anyway, he'd said it was.

We talked about what happened at the club. I told Rocco how I saw Jock get hit, with Lieutenant Maginnis right there, how the hitter went up the fire escape and Maginnis out the alleyway. I told him about the keys missing from the office safe, how the cops found my gun, and how Detective Sergeant Sweeney saw the frame right away. And I told him about the burglary, how a lot of female nudes had been taken off the walls of Jock's studio, the photo-negative filing cabinets had been emptied, and cans of motion picture film stolen.

"You think Maginnis set him up?"

"I do. And I think he may have been trying to set me up at the same time."

"What about this gun of yours—they can tie it into you, or what?"

"It's licensed," I said.

"In your own name?"

"Yes."

"Never, never keep a piece licensed in your own name, Joey. You didn't know that. Now you know."

"Well, I bought it for protection, Rocco. I didn't expect to use it illegally."

"You didn't expect anybody else to use it illegally either. So who was at the club tonight?"

"A few friends of yours," I said. "They got away without being interrogated. Some people Jock and I knew, Father Vito of Actor's Chapel with Hub Grindel and Mady Prevatte—"

"I don't know them," Rocco said.

"Volos was there, with Athena."

"That Greek belly dancer?"

"Egyptian."

"That guy Volos tried to buy the club, did you know?"

"He made Jock and me some offers," I said. "We told him no, thanks. Never discussed it with him."

"He came to me, directly," Rocco said.

"I didn't know that."

"So why the hit? Jealous broad?"

I said, "The female nude shots that someone took off the studio walls could be worth a lot of money to one of those broads, maybe an actress or a high-society type."

"You think Jock was into blackmail?"

"Well, Sergeant Sweeney found ten grand cash hidden in a film pack container in Jock's darkroom. So we have to consider blackmail. But your nephew and I were pretty close, Rocco, and I never had reason to suspect anything. So if he *was* into something, I didn't know about it. But we all have our little secrets."

"Blackmail the only idea you got?"

"Well, I'm wondering what's in those missing cans of movie film."

"You don't know?"

"That's right. I never got into the photography thing

with Jock. He made a lot of shots of me playing the piano, and he used to shoot parties in the club. I've been in his darkroom, but I didn't really know what I was looking at. I do remember the big exhibition prints on the studio walls, of course, but who wouldn't?"

Rocco said, "Blackmail is one of the surest ways to get killed I know of. Anybody who pays off a blackmailer is a patsy. Jock should have known better, but I never thought he had a good head for business."

"Neither have I."

"That's why I got Charlie Green in there taking care of the books, and Dom Ambrosini running the dining room, and George upstairs." `

I hadn't known Uncle Rocco took such a direct hand in our business. I'd thought Jock had hired Dom and George. But then, of course, I'd always left the business end of it up to Jock. I should have guessed, I suppose, because George Patourakis was a professional gambler and so, of course, was Rocco. Not Jock. So Uncle Rocco had surprised me, doubly surprised because George was a Greek. I would have expected Rocco to use a fellow Sicilian or at least an Italian.

I asked, "Have you talked to Charlie Green? Does he know what happened?"

"He isn't home," Rocco said. "I called him a few times. No answer."

I knew about Charlie Green's habits from a couple of talkative hookers he dated, high-class call girls who specialized. Charles Horatio Green was addicted to SM, as it's called nowadays, sadomasochism, whips and bondage. Not that I cared. Whatever turns you on. It's just that I happened to know. So what if he liked having broads tie him up and whip the skin off his ass; it was none off mine.

49

He was still a creative accountant and an unbeatable fixer. But I did think it not unlikely that poor Charlie was tied up in some cathouse, having a ball, though it was none of my business to tell this kind of stuff to Rocco or anybody else.

I said, "Maybe he's out of town on business. He'll get in touch when he hears about Jock."

"It's been on the radio since one o'clock," Rocco said. "And he ain't out of town. His business is my business, and I didn't send him nowhere."

"Maybe he's got a little something going for him on the side?" I suggested.

"Yeah," Rocco said. The tiny gorilla eyes pinned me. Then he blew smoke at the ceiling. "A little something on the side, eh? You wouldn't know, would you?"

"No, Rocco. I was just thinking, some people like to copper their bets."

"He don't have to copper no bets with me, Joey. I take good care of him, like I do all my people. Right, Augie?"

Big Augie, alert by the door, said, "Right, Rocco."

"*You* wouldn't have a little something going for you on the side, would you, Joey?"

"No, Rocco. I just entertain the guests, take my money, and keep my mouth shut. I don't even gamble anymore. Did you know I used to gamble?"

"What about Jock?" he said.

"Come again?"

"Did he have a little something going on the side? Blackmail?"

"I find it hard to believe," I said. "You know, he was a really good photographer. He could have made money at it, but he always said why commercialize if you don't have to."

True. Jock had once rented an art gallery up on Fifty-third Street by the Museum of Modern Art and hung fifty exhibition prints of portraits, people and horses, landscapes, seascapes, and some abstractions. Not for sale. The show cost him a bundle, but all he wanted, he said, was the pleasure of the viewers. The show got good write-ups in the papers, and afterward he received offers from magazine editors, which he turned down, and from book editors, one of which he accepted. During recent weeks he'd been working on a selection of photographs for the book.

I told Rocco about the book. He looked about as understanding as a gorilla.

He said, "How much they paying him for this book of pictures?" I said I didn't know, but I guessed the advance would be enough to cover the cost of preparing the prints, or a little more, a couple of grand, maybe three. "Some business!" he said. He laughed a big-mouth laugh. "Something going for him on the side, right?" He chewed his cigar a little, then said, "Maybe the ten grand that cop found was for the book?"

"Too much," I said. "If he were a famous photographer, maybe. But he wasn't."

"Two, three grand," said Rocco. "And you say it was costing him that much to make the book? What's in it for *him?*"

I said, "Satisfaction."

"With guys like you and him," Rocco said, "it's a good thing I got Charlie Green looking after business." He studied the coal of his cigar, chuckling deep in his chest. "Anything else stolen?" I said no, nothing I knew of. "Ledgers okay?"

I said I didn't know. They weren't in the safe. Maybe

51

Charlie had taken them home to work on them. He often did.

The phone rang. Big Augie picked it up and said hello. He handed it to Rocco.

"Come va?" said Rocco. He watched me as he listened. Covering the mouthpiece with his hand, he said, "It's Dom." I told him to ask Dom if he'd heard from Vickie. "That the dancer used to live with you?" he said. I said she was, and she was supposed to be flying in from Chicago. He asked the question, listened to Dom, looked at me, and shook his head. To Dom he said, "Make sure we got somebody there when you go home. I want it covered at all times, front and back. I'll be leaving here in a little while. Call me on the car phone if there's anything new." He started to hang up, grabbed the phone again, and said, *"Aspetta!* You there, Dom? Listen, you heard from Charlie? . . . Well, ask around. I need to talk to him." He hung up and said, "Lieutenant Maginnis is back at the club. He's got a Commander Fitzroy with him. They took that sergeant off the case. This Commander Fitzroy is from some kind of a homicide task force, Dom says. What's that all about, Joey? You know?"

"I've heard of the Manhattan Homicide Task Force," I said. "If they've taken the case over, maybe somebody has a hook downtown. Too bad about Sergeant Sweeney. He's a bright man, for a cop. He could have run me in for the gun. Any dumb dick would have done it."

"Well, I got worse news for you, Joey. This friend of Maginnis who took over, this Commander Fitzroy, according to Dom, he put out a pick-up-and-hold on you."

"I think I need a lawyer, Rocco."

"You could come to Jersey with us."

"No. I've got to try and find Vickie. Something's wrong.

52

She should have got in touch. She must have left Chicago or she'd have called me. Something happened after she got here. Maybe she's hurt. . . ."

Uncle Rocco replenished our glasses, offered me a fresh Havana, held the match for me.

"So what do you do now?" he asked. "What about Maginnis? What's all this about the keys missing from the safe in the office? And your gun—Jesus Christ!"

"Jock's killer also shot my dog," I said.

"Heidi?"

"I called her Schatzi. It means little sweetheart. I'm going to kill the son of a bitch who did that, Rocco."

"Yeah. I understand how you feel, Joey. So, who you think? Who was Maginnis working with?"

"Maybe not the hitter," I said. "Maginnis set Jock up for the hit, but they were working for somebody else. It has something to do with Jock's pictures. One of the women."

"So what do we do now, Joey?"

"I think you should work on the Maginnis angle," I said. "I'm going to try and locate Vickie."

4

WHEN UNCLE ROCCO AND BIG AUGIE HAD LEFT, I phoned United Airlines and learned that a passenger manifest showed one Victoria Moorcroft had arrived on an early-afternoon flight from Chicago. *Why* hadn't she called? I began to imagine the worst, or what I then thought was the worst. Her taxi could have been in a pileup coming in from the airport. But I realized there must be a dozen hospitals between La Guardia Airport and Manhattan. So I thought of the NYPD, the Bureau of Missing Persons. But I was in no position to make the inquiry since Commander Fitzroy of the Manhattan Homicide Task Force had put out a pick-up-and-hold on me.

I'd been living without Vickie for a couple of months now. I was still very fond of her, and there wasn't much I wouldn't have done for her. We'd met in a simply professional way. Though she was a classical ballerina, she could dance just about anything, and when she spoke to me one night at the club about doing a little number, I let her do it. This was perhaps a year before, when Pal Joey's was a hangout and showcase for performing artists. She asked me if I could improvise jazz variations on Johann Sebastian Bach's "Little Fugue" in G minor. I don't read much music, but it happened I knew the piece and could play it, more or less, by ear. So one afternoon we rehearsed, and that night she did her number. We started it straight, with her doing a classical ballet routine and me playing it pretty much the way Bach wrote it. Then we began to syncopate, and before we were through I was romping Bach with a lot of stride and Vickie was bumping and grinding. We finished where we'd begun, she doing her classical routine and me showing proper respect for Papa Bach. The people loved it and they loved Vickie. She was a lovely girl, slender and graceful, tall and long-legged, the kind of face and figure that classical ballerinas often have, very Russian-looking though her parents were Scotch and Irish and she'd been born and raised in Nova Scotia. She had big brown eyes and swallow's-wing eyebrows, strong cheekbones, a generous mouth, absolutely perfect teeth, and a smile like the dawn of a bright spring morning. Her disposition was amiable, she was affectionate, on occasion passionate, and totally dedicated to the dance and her career.

After her debut that night at Pal Joey's she became a regular act. I put her on salary. Then we found we were spending time after hours together upstairs in my apartment. Little by little she moved in. Then a talent scout caught her act and invited her to go to Chicago for a ballet audition, all expenses paid. She went. She got the contract. And that was that. She moved to Chicago. I missed her at first, of course, for I'd grown used to sleeping with her. But when she moved out, naturally I didn't sleep alone very long, not with all the opportunities in my business. She was always welcome when she'd come back for a few days, and I found consolation when she left again. We remained good friends, good lovers, and though we were not deeply in love, still I was worried about her. So what to do?

I went down to the Central Park entrance of the lobby to see if that big black Cadillac with the New Jersey plates was still parked across the street. It wasn't. I caught a cab and rode it over to the parking lot by the Polyclinic Hospital, where Jock had always put his car. He rented space by the month. He was known to the attendants, and so was I since I often used the car (I had a set of keys). I said good evening to the attendant. He said good morning. He had a radio going in his little office.

I had just stepped past the doorway of the office when he said, "Trouble at the club, Mr. Streeter? I seen all those cops' cars over that way earlier. It's been on the radio . . . about Mr. Alfieri." I had stopped and turned to face him. He was an old gray-haired, light-skinned Negro with a long, drooping hound's face. His name was Oliver. "They say the police are looking for his partner," he went on. "Wanted for questioning, they say on the radio. . . ."

He was leaning against the doorway of the office, watching me and smiling. I pulled the roll out of my pants pocket, peeled off a fifty, and gave it to him. He took it, folding it casually with one hand.

I said, "I'll have to talk to them sooner or later. But first I've got a few things to take care of, Oliver. A few loose ends. I need a little time."

"I understand, Mr. Streeter," he said. "I guess I ain't seen you tonight."

56

"Thanks, Oliver."

"What about Mr. Alfieri's car, sir?"

"Will it make problems for you if I take it?"

"It's paid by the month, you know, and I don't have to check monthly cars in and out. So, officially, he didn't park it here today. Anything else I can do, Mr. Streeter?"

"Thanks again, Oliver. See you."

"Sure, Mr. Streeter. Anytime."

I found the Continental where Jock usually put it, in the middle of the lot under a standing light. I unlocked the trunk. There was nothing but a briefcase. I took it with me into the car. I unlocked the glove compartment and got out the snub-nose Miroku .38, the shoulder holster, and a box of shells. I took off my coat and jacket, strapped on the holster, first adjusting it for size, and slipped the Miroku into it. I put on my jacket and coat again and pocketed the box of shells.

The briefcase was locked and I didn't have the key to it or anything I could use to force it, so I let it wait. I had a hunch what was in it.

As I drove out of the parking lot I could see Oliver in his little office talking on the phone. I mentally crossed my fingers as I drove west and then down to the Port Authority Bus Terminal. I accepted a ticket from the attendant on the ramp and drove up to the parking area on the roof, where I'd told Uncle Rocco that Jock always left the car. By now, no doubt, he wondered what the hell was going on, for he'd surely searched for it.

Sirens began shrieking all over the neighborhood. Good old Oliver, my fifty-dollar friend. I figured if he'd called the law he'd also told them he'd seen me heading west, so they'd calculate I was on my way to the Lincoln Tunnel and New Jersey or else up the West Side Highway toward

57

the George Washington Bridge or even Connecticut. The last place they'd think to look was the parking lot on top of the bus terminal.

It was windy up there in the dawn's early light. And it was Manhattan's quiet time. Or least raucous. For in fact there is no quiet time in Midtown North, the old Eighteenth Precinct, but the hour before dawn has few trucks and buses on the street. Few auto horns. A distant siren whooped like some weird lost bird. From the roof park I could see the smoky red glow above Times Square. Only disaster darkens those lights. The spire of the old Paramount Building towered over the square. Nearer to me was the green glass McGraw-Hill monolith, arrogantly ugly. Westward the street lights of Weehawken shone like strings of glass beads along the top of the palisades. A tug was nosing a barge upstream. Cops' cherry lights were flashing up and down the West Side Highway, and the sound of their sirens wailed across the building tops like small banshees crying, lost in the distance. A gray overcast hid the stars.

I locked the car, took the briefcase with me, and rode the elevator down to the lower level, where I phoned Matt Griffin at the Hotel Commodore. True, I could have gone back to the Plaza, but since I didn't understand Uncle Rocco's role in this night's happenings, I thought the Commodore might be more discreet. He didn't know I had a room there.

When I got Matt on the phone he told me the detectives had already checked on me and found that I'd registered, all right, but they'd also gone up to 1115 and found I wasn't there. Fine, I thought. Then they won't be expecting to see me at the Commodore. I told Matt to meet me at the service entrance just off the Grand Concourse in

Grand Central Station. Then I doubled back by way of the underground pedestrian passage that leads from the Port Authority Bus Terminal to Times Square, and there I took the shuttle train to Grand Central. Whoever laid out midtown Manhattan must have had a criminal mind. You can go just about anywhere you like and never stick your head aboveground. Sherlock Holmes couldn't find Professor Moriarty in New York City, and vice versa.

Matt was waiting for me at the Commodore service entrance. He had to be, since that door was kept locked from the inside. He took me up to 1115 again, and on the way I gave him some money to buy me a fresh shirt, boxer shorts, stretch socks, and sunglasses. And I gave him a double sawbuck for himself. He said he'd take care of everything as soon as the stores opened. I asked him to get me something meanwhile to open Jock's briefcase. He came back in a few minutes with a set of picklocks. We opened the briefcase, and he left. I double-locked the door and latched the chain.

The missing cross-index cards to the negative files, both stills and movies, were in the briefcase. According to the cards, Jock had made five short motion pictures and a number of "loops." The movies were *Pickup on Swing Street,* with Hub Grindel and Mady Prevatte; *The Champ,* with Chico Grande and Honey Wing; *Danse du Ventre,* with Athena Hosnani doing a solo bit; *Sweet Life,* with a large cast of pseudonymous Times Square hookers and hustlers; and *The Kama Sutra Tango,* with Licia and Lucio Garay.

The title cards were dated. Apparently Jock had made *Pickup on Swing Street* first, on New Year's Eve and the following day, according to a note on the card. His second movie was *Danse du Ventre,* made two weeks later. *The*

59

Kama Sutra Tango was third, then *The Champ,* and finally *Sweet Life.* This last had been completed only a week before he was murdered. I had no idea what the sequence meant. I hadn't known Jock was into porn movies at all. Anyway, I couldn't assume that all these films were porn, but I was sure about *Sweet Life.* The title card listed the performers and some of them were well known around Times Square.

Three of these girls were also in Jock's loops, according to their index cards: Marie La Touche, Judy Piper, and Olga Herasimchuk, afternoon shake dancers in the topless bars, ladies of the evening, part-time porn-movie actresses. I knew them well, all three. Or so I thought.

As to the nude stills, the cross-index included three other performers from the movies: Mady Prevatte, Honey Wing, and of course Athena Hosnani, whose nude photo had been found by Sergeant Sweeney in Jock's wallet.

The rest of the index cards concerned only the usual portraits of people and animals, landscapes and seascapes, and so forth.

I took the cards that referred to the movies and loops and nude stills and stowed them in an inside pocket of my jacket. The others I left in the briefcase and closed it. The movies' title cards had each performer's name and address and phone number. I could use this information. Loop performers, however, rarely have permanent addresses. Marie, Judy, and Olga had been working at the Bon Bon Bar, a topless joint. I wondered if they were still there.

I recalled that a number of the people in the movies had been at Pal Joey's the night before: handsome Hub Grindel and socialite Mady Prevatte, welterweight contender Chico Grande and starlet Honey Wing, of course Athena

Hosnani, and the Garay twins. None of the loop girls had been at the club, so far as I knew.

Funny thing about those girls in the loops: they weren't your common, garden-variety hookers. I mean the three I knew, Marie, Judy, and Olga. They worked and lived together. Tight as triplets. They were fairly bright about some things, quick on the uptake, skilled in the boudoir arts. Marie La Touche was a truly red-haired, green-eyed colleen from a village on the Jersey shore, née Mary Alice Mooney, who'd come to New York (she said) after a glamorous debut as an actress in the Toms River High School senior play. In New York she'd never got past the theatrical agents' casting couches. Judy Piper was a bed-luscious Roman beauty from Bensonhurst in Brooklyn, née Judy Scandale (so *she* said), bright enough in a way, and true blue, but very dumb about men (she claimed) and always being manipulated by some psychopathic pimp. Olga Herasimchuk was a brown-eyed, curly-haired natural blond, and Olga Herasimchuk was her right name. Had to be. With a name like that, why would she lie? She'd come uptown from the Lower East Side, graduated in psychology at New York University (*she* said), and was a rampant nympho. The latter I believed. I didn't see how any of these girls could have been involved in Jock's murder. If the ten thousand dollars in used tens and twenties that Sergeant Sweeney had said he'd found in a film can in Jock's darkroom was blackmail money, it hadn't come from any of the hookers in those porn loops. Where would a poor whore get that kind of money? So who then?

Mady Prevatte, the socialite with acting ambitions? She had a town house on Park Avenue, a *pied-à-terre* in the Sherry-Netherland, a mansion at Montauk, another in the Poconos on two hundred acres of virgin forest land. She skied at Gstaad, hunted boars in Yugoslavia, shot grouse in the Hebrides, staged spectacular parties in Rome. She could pay ten grand in blackmail out of her pin money. If Jock had tapped *her* for a mere ten thousand, he'd asked far too little.

Honey Wing? I couldn't see her paying blackmail. I thought she might even welcome this kind of publicity, which was about the only way she'd ever get any. A party girl, a chippy, a nobody who claimed to be an actress, she'd come over from Saigon with the last refugees. A bleached-blond Eurasian, what kind of actress had she been in Saigon? Well, she sure as hell was in a movie now, with star billing. As for the ten thousand dollars, she couldn't raise more than a hundred if she worked all night.

Athena Hosnani? She might put down ten grand if she had it. I thought she'd hardly want Gentleman John Volos, the Patriarch of Chelsea, to know about her naked *Danse du Ventre* movie. On the other hand, I hadn't seen it myself, so I was unable to say if it was blackmail material. According to her index card it was a solo act, apparently her regular belly dance. But no doubt in the nude. After all, there was that nude shot in Jock's wallet. But where would an Egyptian belly dancer get ten thousand dollars? From Gentleman John Volos.

The tiny twins, Licia and Lucio Garay? Sure, they'd pay blackmail if they had the money. When they did their "Kama Sutra Tango" act in their usual costume, both of them in white tie and tails, it didn't matter how many *Kama Sutra* positions they took while doing their tango steps. But if the movie indexed as *The Kama Sutra Tango* showed them naked, as I assumed it must, fornicating while dancing . . . ? In words of one syllable, wow. Let the word get around and they'd never see the inside of the Empire Room at the Waldorf. They'd be lucky to get dates in the performers' limbo, Long Island roadhouses. *They'd* pay ten grand to keep it quiet if they'd been dumb fool enough to perform for Jock Alfieri's movie camera in the first place. And apparently they had. But where would they get ten big ones? Nowhere, that's where. Unless maybe their impresario came up with it. I thought he could easily have that kind of money. Candido Valentino was known as Candy the Dandy for good reason, being a snowbird himself and candyman to a lot of moneyed people in the entertainment world and on Park Avenue.

As for the men in these movies, would they be likely to pay blackmail? Hub Grindel? Well, he did have serious career ambitions, and a porn flick wouldn't help him get ahead in the theater, or even in Hollywood. As for Chico Grande, where would he get ten grand? He'd never in his life cleared that much on a fight. His manager, Doubles Gross, kept him in pocket money. Chico was a chronic loser. Not for nothing was he known as Canvasback Grande.

Then it occurred to me that the ten thousand dollars might have come from more than one source, and all bets were off.

By the time I'd gone through the index cards and considered the more obvious angles, it was 6 A.M. I switched on the room radio and caught the early news report. The first item was last night's murder at Pal Joey's. After reciting the police version of the facts, the announcer said that Detective Commander Malcolm Fitzroy of the Manhattan Homicide Task Force had escalated his pick-up-and-hold on jazz pianist Joe Streeter to a warrant for murder.

"The wanted man may be armed and dangerous," said the newscaster.

So I checked Jock's little Miroku .38, emptied the cylinder, worked the action a few times, and reloaded. Commander Fitzroy had it right. The wanted man was armed and dangerous.

Then I turned in for some shut-eye, but sleep was a long time coming, and when it did, I slept very lightly, half-awake, dreaming of Vickie. In my dream she was playing with Schatzi in Central Park. It was in Sheep Meadow and they were wrestling in the grass, rolling over and over. . . .

❧ 5 ❧

I DREAMED OF VICKIE and Schatzi until ten o'clock, when Matt brought the shirt, shorts, and socks. And sunglasses. He'd also thought to bring a razor, shaving cream, toothbrush, and a tube of Colgate's. He hadn't had much sleep himself, but he was a wiry old guy and very spry despite his maybe seventy years. I had him order up some breakfast, and then we listened to the WCBS news spots while I shaved and showered.

The murder warrant was still out. The radio announcer didn't mention Jock's car. Either the cops hadn't found it, or they weren't saying anything about it. Could be they didn't want to tip me that Oliver at the Polyclinic parking lot had blown the whistle. I didn't know he had, I just thought so. Or could be they were looking for the Continental in Jersey or even up in Connecticut.

Other news concerned a Manhattan murder that had occurred between 7 and 8 A.M. The victim was Milton Cohen, whom I'd known slightly, the manager of Petrocelli Products, a wholesale meat-packaging firm down in Chelsea which supplied Pal Joey's. Though the radio announcer didn't make the connection—and possibly the cops hadn't yet made it either—Petrocelli Products was an enterprise in which Uncle Rocco Lucarelli had an interest. No cash had been stolen, only three trucks loaded with merchandise. Men wearing stocking masks and speaking with heavy foreign accents had pulled the caper.

I tried to add it up. Item—someone went to a lot of trouble to frame me for Jock's murder. Item—Vickie disappeared sometime during the afternoon or evening, probably the afternoon. If she'd had the afternoon free after arriving at La Guardia, I was sure she'd have phoned me. Item—the managers of two of Uncle Rocco's businesses were murdered and merchandise stolen. Jock had been the manager, or at any rate the nominal manager, of Pal Joey's. How could all this tie in with the theft of still photos, negatives, and porn movies? Were these negatives and stills and movies to be considered merchandise? Yes, in two ways: Porn movies and loops are certainly marketable, and somebody had paid the ten thousand dollars for *something*. But would the same person or persons also take three truckloads of packaged meats?

Matt hung in with me while I ate breakfast and we listened to the radio news. Then he came up with an idea that seemed to make sense. I'd told him about Uncle Rocco's involvement in Pal Joey's and in Petrocelli Products.

"What if it isn't the same people who did both jobs?" he said. "Rocco Lucarelli being in both businesses doesn't have to prove anything, does it?"

"Too much coincidence if there's no connection," I said.

"Maybe not," he went on. "Look at it this way. The

news of Jock's murder has been on the radio all night. Someone hears it, decides to raid that meat-packaging outfit, using Jock's murder as a kind of smoke screen, a cover, to throw the cops off, right? I mean, once the cops make the Lucarelli connection they'll try to tie the two capers together, right? And if there's really no connection, the bulls are off on a wild-goose chase."

"Far out," I told him. "Too far out."

"Well, murder's pretty far out, isn't it?"

I had to agree. But what about Vickie? How did her disappearance tie in? Maybe it didn't?

"Two things I've got to do," I said. "First, find Vickie. Then find Jock's killer."

Matt said, "Vickie?"

I told him about her disappearance. He'd known her well. Before she took that ballet job in Chicago, she'd often been present at after-hours jam sessions in my pad. He and Vickie had been fond of each other and she'd always looked out for him at the jam sessions, made sure he took something to eat, brewed tea for him.

I said, "Maybe when I find her I'll know the rest of it —why Jock was killed, the Petrocelli caper. . . ."

"Any ideas?"

"Not a damn one."

"I have," he said. "Take it in order, Joey. From what you tell me, it looks to me like the *first* thing happened, Vickie disappears, right? *Then* Jock gets killed and his photo stuff gets stolen. *Then* the raid on Petrocelli Products. In that order, right? So if all three are connected in some way, it begins with Vickie's disappearance. *She* could be the key to your problem, Joey. You dig what I'm saying?"

I said, "Yeah, well, the first thing I'm going to do is find her, or try to. The rest can wait."

"You don't dig it, Joey, what I'm saying."

I did, though. He was saying Vickie was the answer to my emotional needs. I didn't think she was, though I liked her very much and always enjoyed her company in and out of bed.

But I had to agree that if she was involved somehow in last night's events, she was the key to the reason they happened. A very big *if*, it seemed to me. But the only *if*, for the moment.

I told Matt, "I dig it, Pops. But I don't agree with all of it. Which doesn't matter, because, like I said, the first thing I do is find Vickie. Okay?"

Matt said, "Anything I can do, anything at all—I'd lay down my life for that girl. She's a pure jewel."

"I know," I said, getting annoyed.

"No, you don't, son," he said. "You never did. You always took her for granted. I could see it myself. You let her get away, Joey."

"She had her career to think of."

Lame? I know it. I didn't *let* her get away. I just didn't try to stop her when she went. But it's true, I always took her for granted. I'm a heel, a cad, a blackguard, but I simply was never in love with Vickie. Nor she with me, so far as I knew. It was a liaison between consenting adults. Old Matt was playing Cupid. Or he wanted her himself. Maybe both, for he was a complicated old man.

He said, "You young studs are all alike. No heart."

I said, "I'm not so young."

"Don't tell *me* that, Joey."

"Sorry."

"So where do you start looking for her?"

68

"I guess wherever I find Mady Prevatte. For a start."

"That Texas oil heiress, Park Avenue socialite?"

"The same. And Hub Grindel."

"Part-time actor, full-time easy rider. Why would Vickie get in touch with them and not with you if she was coming in to spend a few days with you, like you say?"

"Well, if for some reason she'd been unable to get in touch with me during the afternoon or evening, or last night until, say, three-thirty this morning, she'd have no way of reaching me after I left the club. As you know, I've been out of touch. So she might have called one of our mutual friends, and why not Mady?"

"Who else?"

"Maybe Honey Wing."

"That hotsy-totsy? I can't see our Vickie getting in touch with a chippy like that."

"Honey's not your common chippy," I said. "She may be trash, but she's an honest whore."

"Anybody else?"

"I don't know. Maybe the Garay twins."

"For God's sake, what would she want with *them?* No, man, you're off on the wrong track."

"There's no harm in checking them out. They know Vickie."

"Waste of time, Joey. Who else?"

"Candy Valentino, Doubles Gross, Chico Grande . . ."

"A snowbird, a shylock, a punching bag."

"And I'll try Father Vito."

"Now you're starting to make sense, buddy. If Vickie got in touch with anybody but you, it has to be Father Vito."

"I'll call him," I said.

"Don't use the room phone," Matt said. "Who knows, the cops could still be rooting around the hotel. Better just go to Actor's Chapel."

I'd finished my breakfast, so I brushed my teeth and put on Jock's shoulder holster, sticking his Miroku .38 in the scabbard. Matt asked to see it. I handed it to him.

"Where'd you find this piece of junk?" he said.

"What do you mean, junk? It was Jock's. He kept it in the glove compartment of his car."

Matt broke the gun, cocked it, and said, "Look at this. Firing pin mounted on a swivel, for God's sake. It could break off."

I hadn't told him about my own gun. I told him now. He said it looked like a frame. I told him Sergeant Sweeney thought so too. Then I told him the whole story: how I'd happened to witness Jock's murder, with Lieutenant Maginnis standing by, how Sergeant Sweeney had found my gun where it was supposed to be, in the drawer of the nightstand by my bed, three rounds gone, one shell on the ground in the patio near Jock's body. And how someone had shot my dog.

"What a weird frame," Matt said. "Why would you shoot Jock and your dog and then stash your piece in your own apartment?"

"Sweeney called it a double frame," I said. "He thought unless I was crazy I wouldn't put a double frame around myself."

"Sweeney, eh? So who's this Commander Fitzroy they're talking about on the radio?"

"He's Manhattan Homicide Task Force. Looks like Maginnis brought him in somehow. They pulled Sweeney off the case, put out a pick-up-and-hold on me, then made it

70

wanted for murder. I guess they figure my gun's all they need. They don't have to show motive."

"Dear God! What's happening, Joey? Who's out to get you?"

"No idea. I'm not sure anyone is."

I told him the rest of it, the nude stills, porno movies. I told him about the ten thousand dollars and how the nude stills were missing along with film cans of porn flicks and the file of negatives. I also told him about the cross-index file cards that I'd found in Jock's briefcase.

"So it looks like Jock was into blackmail," I said, "and somebody didn't get what he paid for. But that doesn't explain the hit on Uncle Rocco's meat-packaging plant down in Chelsea this morning."

"It might," Matt said, "if Rocco's involved in the black-mail."

"Good point," I said. "But it doesn't explain someone putting a frame around *me.*"

"Maybe someone thinks you're involved . . . ?"

"And Vickie?"

"I have to admit that stumps me, Joey. So you start by trying to find her, like you said. Anything I can do . . . One thing I *can* do—I can get you a good gun, something that'll really work when you need it."

"Don't worry," I said. "Jock told me he'd fired this piece a lot, shooting at beer cans, and apparently it never broke down."

"Pray God it doesn't."

I left Jock's briefcase with Matt, since I already had the important index cards in my pocket.

As I went down the back stairway, a sudden thought nearly blew my mind. If there's a murder warrant out on

71

you, plus the belief that you are armed and dangerous, as the radio news announcer had said, the cops would feel the urge to shoot first. With this nice thought in mind, I began my search for Vickie.

⚜ 6 ⚜

I CAUGHT A CAB at the Commodore's side entrance on the Park Avenue ramp, careful not to take one with the Civilian Radio Patrol emblem on its door. An obvious gumshoe at the exit scrutinized me, but didn't make me. Homburg, chesterfield, and sunglasses are an effective disguise for a man who never wears sunglasses and is known to always go bareheaded. And if the fuzz were looking for a man with white hair they just might miss me—my sideburns are still dark gray.

I told the cabby to head up Park Avenue and over Forty-ninth Street, and on Forty-ninth east of Seventh Avenue in front of the big White Rose bar I saw a pair of characters I knew well. Light-skinned spades from uptown. Ex-entertainers. I thought they might know something or be able to help in some way. One was dirty-talking Sylvester Beamish, a little old hoofer who'd been known as Specks when he still wore glasses, before he went stone blind with glaucoma. He was also known as

73

Mister Magoo because of the way he'd come up close to you and try to see you. Before he went completely blind he once danced off the apron of the Apollo stage and fell into a kettledrum, a historical fact though he will always deny it. Now he doesn't dance except once in a while a little soft-shoe at McAnn's bar when he's high and the boys talk him into it. The other character was his buddy, known as Nickels Detroit. No one knew him by any other name. He was a silent man, said hardly a word, hailed from Detroit, and eked out his living by dealing five-dollar bags of reefer. He was an old guy like Specks, and he'd been a hoofer too, but now his legs were crippled, swollen like enormous sausages from a series of strokes, which had also impaired his speech. Though he never talked much, he could see all right, so he got around by leaning on Specks. A Biblical pair, the halt leading the blind. They were both on welfare, or some kind of social security, so with a few steady bucks coming in from the nickel bags of grass they were able to stay consistently juiced, and other old-timers, musicians and singers and dancers who still got a gig now and then, laid a few skins on them from time to time. Also, Specks had a good head for numbers —telephone digits and street addresses—so if somebody wanted something like girls or guns or dope or a bottle on Sunday, he could connect him up, and this small service was worth a single or a deuce.

I stopped the cab and told the driver to wait. I got out and took Specks and Detroit into a doorway next to the big White Rose. It was the doorway of a cathouse. Two broads in hot pants were on their way upstairs with a john who looked like a vice cop. He might get laid free, he might also take their money, and he might get cut. Some of these *filles de joie* carry razors or other blades in their handbags. Or guns.

Specks had a perfect memory for voices, and when I spoke he said, "Hey, motherfucker! Somebody been looking for you all morning."

He had only one dirty word in his vocabulary, and he used it on everyone but the ladies. Nobody gave it a second thought.

I said, "Who's looking for me, Specks?"

"Somebody who wants to talk to you, motherfucker." He held out his hand, peering up at me with his blind eyes and grinning. I got out the roll and slapped a sawbuck into his palm. He said, "What is it, motherfucker, one skinny single?"

Detroit mumbled, "It's a five, Specks." Then to me Detroit said, "Father Vito wants you should call him." I thanked him and he said, "Listen, man, I got some fine puff, the bestest."

That was about as much as Detroit ever said. To do him a favor, I gave him a five and took a bag, a tiny manila envelope about the size of a Christmas postage stamp. You might get two joints out of one of his nickels if you rolled them thin as matchsticks. I wouldn't bother.

I asked them if they remembered Victoria Moorcroft. They did. They hadn't known her, though they'd known she was my girl, and of course Specks had never seen her dance, but he'd heard, and a good hustler remembers everything. Anything at all could be worth money.

"She's missing," I told them. "She flew in from Chicago yesterday afternoon to spend a few days with me, but she never got to the club and I haven't heard from her."

Specks said, "Think it ties in with Jock's murder? We

was next door at McAnn's last night when the pigs came."

"I don't know what to think," I said. "What's the word? Anything at all?"

"They say Mike Maginnis had something to do with it. Somebody seen him go into the alley by Pal Joey's and come out again in a little while. It was about that time, they say."

"I don't know," I said. "Maginnis was there, all right. I don't know for sure what he was doing there."

"The laws got a murder warrant out on you, mother-fucker."

"That's this Commander Fitzroy, and maybe Maginnis. There was a Sergeant Al Sweeney on the case. Looks like they took him off it. Sweeney didn't think I killed Jock. He could see the frame. I'd like to talk to Sweeney. Pass the word, will you?"

"We don't talk to cops, motherfucker."

"Sure you do, Specks."

He looked up at me as if he could see me, or through me. He was remembering that I knew Detroit's grass dealer was Detective Dan Lee, known as Dan the Man, of course.

"That's different," Specks said. "Dan's a vice cop."

"The worst," I said, "next to narcs. At least Al Sweeney's into something clean like homicide. So pass the word. He should get in touch. Father Vito will take a message."

I laid a sawbuck on him, another on his partner.

Detroit said, "Thanks, Mr. Streeter."

But Specks just grinned up at me, saying nothing.

I got back in the cab and told the driver to keep going west. He headed across the upper end of Times Square. It was crowded with the usual out-of-towners, uptowners, downtowners, hookers, pickpockets, and plainclothesmen. On the northwest corner of Forty-ninth Street and Broadway a tall, gaunt sky pilot known as Hellfire Henry was standing on a milk-bottle crate, looking like an early Christian martyr and haranguing the crowd about Heaven and Hell while his confederate, a clubfooted light Negro known as Badfoot George, was dipping the gentlemen's wallets. A trio of plainclothes cops were watching, waiting for their cut. A vice cop was haggling with a hooker in the doorway of the old Jack Dempsey's, half a block up the street. A gaggle of Krishnavites were prancing and chanting by the statue of Father Duffy just below the discount ticket booth. Three big-hatted, tight-assed pimps in ankle-length phony-fur coats were slapping hands and laughing the big spade laugh at the Krishnavites. It was a normal noonday on old Times Square.

❧ 7 ☙

WHEN I PAID OFF THE CABBY in front of Actor's Chapel, which is on Forty-ninth Street a half block west of Broadway, there were no cops on the block, unless two old winos across the street were cops. I didn't think so. The fuzz would be up on Fiftieth Street by the club. I rang the rectory bell, and presently Father Vito himself opened.

"Come in, quick!" he said. I stepped inside and he peered up and down the street before he shut the door. "I've been looking everywhere for you," he said. "Vickie's been calling me. She wants to talk to you."

Father Vito Caracciola was a small, fat, one-eared, happy Jesuit from Brooklyn. He always wore a smile, or almost always. He'd lost the ear in a fight when he was a boy at Saint Joseph's Academy. An Irish kid had chewed it off, and thirty years later Vito was still doing penance for breaking the little mick's back and paralyzing him for life. A heavy load on Vito's conscience, still he smiled. But he wasn't smiling now. His bright brown eyes looked sad as a spaniel's. His mouth was drawn down with worry.

"Where is she?" I asked him. "Is she all right?"

"Come upstairs," he said. "She's due to call again in a few minutes." He led the way. When we were in his study, at the back of the building, I went to the windows. You could see the patio of Pal Joey's. I was looking for cops, of course, but there were none. I figured they'd be in front of the club or inside. "She's been calling me every hour on the hour since five this morning," Vito said. "She won't explain, says she can't come to the chapel, won't reveal her whereabouts, and will only talk to you. We have a few minutes until she's due to call again. I'd like you to brief me on what's been happening, Joe. Can you?"

"Part of it," I said. "Part of it's confessional material, but it's not *my* confession. It involves some of your communicants, people I've seen here at mass."

"Just tell me what you can," he said.

I told him the story without revealing the names of the people involved in the nude still photos and the porn movies. Two of them, Mady Prevatte and Hub Grindel, had been with him at the club last night. They and the Garay twins occasionally attended mass at the chapel. Also Chico Grande. I wasn't a communicant myself, couldn't make a sincere act of contrition, but I did attend mass two or three times a week.

Vito thought over what I'd told him, then he got out a bottle of Barolo and poured us each a small glass of the rich, dark wine.

"Blackmail," he said. "That ten thousand dollars . . . I'd never have figured Jock for that kind of scam. Is the uncle involved?"

"In the blackmail?" I said. "I doubt it. The porn movies, yes, I think so, though he denies it. But it seems to go

79

deeper. There's the caper at Petrocelli Products this morning, one of Uncle Rocco's businesses. Have you heard the radio?"

"Yes."

The phone rang. The clock on Vito's desk said one, straight up. He picked up the phone and handed it to me without a word.

I said, "Vickie?"

I held the phone away from my ear so Vito could listen.

Vickie said, "Joey?" Her voice was quavery, trembling on the edge of hysteria. "Oh, Joey!"

I said, "Are you all right, honey? Where are you?"

"I can't tell you. They won't let me. I'm all right, so far, but listen, Joey, they've got me tied up. There's somebody holding the phone for me. They want something. They say Jock had some motion picture films, and they want them or they'll do something horrible to me. They've already done it to somebody else. They made me watch."

I said, "Who?"

A hoarse, masculine voice came on the line then, saying, "No more questions, Streeter. We want those films and all the copies. You hear? *All* the copies. Or we take the broad apart. You tell Rocco. Got it?"

I said yes. Vickie cried out. Someone hung up.

When real trouble is going down, confessional matters have no privilege in my opinion, so I told Vito the rest of it, naming names. He looked as if I'd slipped a knife between his ribs.

His voice was tight as he said, "How do you *know* these persons are involved in the pornographic films?"

"I have Jock's cross-index card file."

I handed the cards to him. He studied them.

"Incredible," he murmured. "I thought I knew Hub,

80

and Mady, the Garay twins. I never knew them at all."

"Then you don't confess them?"

"Obviously. But they receive communion here, so someone must be confessing them. How many of these movies are they involved in?" He studied the cards again. "One film for Hub and Mady," he said, "one for the Garays, one for Chico Grande. I don't know these others —Athena Hosnani, Honey Wing. . . ."

I told him Athena was an Egyptian belly dancer, protegée of Iovannis "Gentleman John" Volos, danced at one of his clubs, the Eurydice, and Honey Wing was a Eurasian refugee from Saigon who claimed to be an actress and was in fact the poopsie-doll of Ruby Porcelain, the Broadway producer. He never did much producing, but managed a lot of pimping.

Vito said, "Which one of these people would pay ten thousand dollars blackmail? That one might lead you to the person holding Vickie. That's your first problem."

"It is," I said. "Also, not getting shot by the cops while I'm looking for her. But you've asked the right question, I think. Which of these people could, or would, pay blackmail, and even murder the blackmailer?"

"I can't believe Mady Prevatte would do it," Vito said. "But she's the only one of them I know who could pay that kind of money. And she'd have reason to. She's engaged to marry Count Carlo Gesualdo. He comes from an ancient Italian line—no money but a lot of nobility. He couldn't marry her if it became known that she'd performed in a pornographic film."

"Why not, Father?"

"The disgrace . . ."

"But Mady has the money. You say this count has none. Or is he marrying her for love?"

"I really don't know," Vito said. "Have you a cigar, Joe? I'm fresh out." I gave him one. We lit up. "I can't understand," he said, "how she'd get involved in the first place. Why would she, Joe? You're more worldly-wise than I. Can you explain it? Was she forced somehow?"

"Well, they weren't *all* forced, Father."

"No. I suppose not. Then why? Could this card file be in error, Joe?"

"I doubt it. Whoever is holding Vickie wants those films. I'd say the cards, or at least some of them, are accurate. Father, I don't give a damn about those films or who performed in them or why, and if they don't lead me to Vickie they mean absolutely nothing to me."

"I understand, Joe. And you're right. But apparently you've got to get the films in order to help Vickie. And you've got to start with Rocco Lucarelli, according to the man on the phone."

"Okay. I'll call Rocco now," I said.

I picked up the phone and started dialing the Lucarelli residence in Short Hills.

"Just like that?" Vito said. "You know Lucarelli's number?"

"I've been to the house with Jock many times."

"Then I'd say Vickie's kidnappers know this, and they don't know how to reach Lucarelli directly. Which tells us something."

"What?"

"They need you as the contact man."

"I'm not so sure," I said. "Maybe they do know how to reach Rocco, but for some reason they don't want to do it directly."

Big Augie Benedetto answered the phone with a gruff hello, and that was all.

82

I said, "It's Harold Williams. I'd like to speak with Mr. Lucarelli, please."

"Who?"

"Harold Williams, from the Hotel Plaza. Remember?"

"I'll tell him," Big Augie said.

Then Uncle Rocco came on, growling, "Where you calling from?"

"Public phone booth," I said. "Can I talk?"

"Better meet. How come that car ain't where you said?"

"It is."

"We didn't see it."

"It's there," I said. "How soon can we meet?"

"One hour."

"Where?"

"Where the car is, if that's where it is."

"It's there," I said. "See you in one hour. Better hurry. I've got bad news."

I hung up.

Vito said, "Public phone booth? Harold Williams?"

I said, "Rocco understands the Harold Williams bit. The public phone booth was to protect you, Father. I wouldn't want to get you involved."

"It's my job to get involved, Joe."

"Sorry."

"Would you like me to go with you to the meeting?"

"No, thanks. I appreciate the offer. A priest might make Rocco feel guiltier than he already is. Just get me a cab when it's time to go. I don't have to leave for about forty minutes."

"Then the meeting isn't far?"

"The parking lot on the roof of the Port Authority Bus Terminal."

83

"A highly exposed position," Vito said.

"Rocco's idea," I said. "I wouldn't argue such a small point with him. Let him win the battles; I'll win the war."

"Strong talk, Joe. Expecting trouble?"

"With Rocco? He *is* trouble."

❧ 8 ❧

WHEN IT WAS TIME TO GO, I waited inside the street door while Vito hailed a cab. A Checker stopped. Vito held the taxi door for me. I looked quickly up and down the street, then hurried across the sidewalk and ducked into the cab. He shut the door. I rolled the window down.

"Tell Vickie I've gone to meet the gentleman in question," I said. "Tell her I'll call you as soon as I've seen him."

"Take care, will you?"

I told the cabby to take me to Ninth Avenue and Fortieth Street. As we passed the Ninth Avenue entrance to the Port Authority Terminal, which is between Fortieth and Forty-first Streets, it seemed to me the NYPD's entire plainclothes force was there. So I had the driver hang a left on Fortieth and I entered the building on that side. I took the elevator to the roof. During midday hours very few people are up there, but the roof is packed solid with commuters' cars.

Apparently the cops hadn't found the Continental, for I saw no stakeout. So I unlocked the driver's door and got in. I left the other doors locked. I took out my key case and removed the car key and stuck it in the ignition lock.

In about five minutes Uncle Rocco's black Eldorado came cruising along. Big Augie Benedetto was driving. He had another man in the front seat with him. Rocco was alone in the back. Big Augie parked just behind the Continental and I got out. Rocco opened his door. I climbed in.

The man in front with Big Augie got out and went over to the Continental and began changing the license plates. The way Rocco's car was parked, no one would notice what the man was doing. Anyway, there weren't more than a handful of people scattered around the roof, getting in or out of their cars, paying no attention to anybody.

Rocco said, "How come I didn't see Jock's car last night?" He offered me a Havana. I took it and lit it. "Was it right where it is now? Maybe you moved it?"

I said, "Look, Rocco, there isn't much time, so let's get down to business. It's about Jock's pornographic movies. Have you got them, any of them, originals or copies?"

"No. Why?"

"Someone's holding Vickie for ransom. The price is those movies, all of them, all copies."

"Vickie?"

"Victoria Moorcroft."

"I remember her."

"Well, she was flying in yesterday to spend a few days with me, but somebody snatched her. I got a phone call from her about an hour ago, but she couldn't tell me who's got her or where she's being held. All I know is I need those films or she's in deep trouble."

"I wish I could help you, Joey."

"Sure you can't?"

"Positive. Who you think got her?"

"No idea, Rocco. Could be somebody involved in those porn movies."

"So who?"

"You don't know?"

"That's right."

"I thought maybe you and Jock were in the skin-flick business together."

"No way, Joey. But I think you're right—whoever got her is somebody involved in those movies. When you find out who, come to me. I'll take care of it. I want the man who killed Jock."

"Have you heard from Charlie Green?"

"No. You?"

"No."

"Where'd you get this phone call from the girl?"

"Actor's Chapel. You know Father Vito Caracciola?"

"Heard of him. How's he figure in this?"

"Of all the people Vickie and I know, he's the straight one. So she got in touch with me through him. You can do the same. He's in the book. Just look up Actor's Chapel. I won't be there, but he'll take a message.

"How much does he know?"

"Nothing."

The man who'd been changing the plates on Jock's car was finished now. He came back and reported to Rocco.

"You got the parking ticket?" Rocco asked me.

I gave it to him without thinking. Then I thought about it. If I couldn't think faster than that, I might not live long enough to do much more thinking. But Rocco just took the ticket and gave it to his man. Then he asked for the car keys.

"In the ignition," I said.

Rocco didn't say anything. His man got into the Continental and drove away toward the ramp. The man might notice the date and time on the ticket when he paid the charges on the way down the ramp. But that was for the future.

"Now what are you going to do?" Rocco asked.

I said, "I'd like to start with the people who performed in those porn flicks."

"You know who they are?"

"No, Rocco. I was hoping you could tell me."

"Like I said, Joey, I don't know nothing about it."

"What about Charlie Green?"

"He wouldn't be into nothing like that, Joey. But I'll ask if he knows anything when he shows up. I got people looking for him. He didn't get back to his apartment last night, and he hasn't been to his office today. He must of took a little vacation for himself."

"What about Petrocelli Products?"

"Just a ripoff. Hoods."

"No connection?"

"With Jock's murder? How you figure that, Joey?"

"Well, the nominal manager of Pal Joey's was your nephew. He gets killed. His photographic materials are stolen. Then the manager of Petrocelli Products gets killed. Three trucks of merchandise are stolen. No connection? You're into both businesses, Rocco. That looks like a connection to me."

"No way, Joey."

"The people who snatched Vickie think you have the missing cans of movie film. They told me to talk to you."

"Joey, they're wrong. Naturally they think I was into all

that stuff with Jock, him being my nephew, but I
you, Joey, on my mother's grave, I didn't have no
do with no sex movies."

"If you say so, Rocco, then that's that. I'd bett
on."

I started to open the car door. Rocco's right hand
into his jacket by the left shoulder. I saw the gu
coming out and reached for my little Miroku .38
because Rocco was sitting on my left I had my gu
before he could swing his around. He stopped.

"Hey, Joey!" he said, trying to smile. "I was just g
to offer you the loan of my piece, and here you go
draw on me. What's the matter, Joey?"

"Put it away, Rocco."

"Sure. I was just . . ."

I had one eye on Big Augie in the front seat. I saw
right arm move. He was opening his jacket. I remer
bered he was a lefty, but I couldn't see what his left han
was doing. I figured he was going for his gun.

I told him, "Hold it right there, Augie. I'll blow you
head off."

He didn't move.

Rocco said, "Now, Joey . . ."

"Put the gun away," I said.

He did. I shifted my gun to my left hand and opened
the car door.

Rocco said, "I don't know what's come over you, Joey."

I had to laugh, but it didn't sound much like a laugh.

I said, "I'll tell you what's come over me, Rocco. My best
girl gets snatched, my partner gets killed, somebody
frames me for it, and there's a murder warrant out on me.
That's what's come over me. And that isn't all. Good old

Uncle Rocco pulls a gun on me."

"Forget it, Joey. I wasn't pulling no gun on you. I was just—"

"You said. I heard."

"Joey, how come you had Jock's parking ticket?"

"He gave it to me yesterday afternoon so I could run out to La Guardia and pick up Vickie when she arrived. Only she didn't call when she got in, so I still had the ticket after Jock was shot."

"Funny," Rocco said. "We come up here and looked all over this goddamn roof. We even looked on the lower parking floors. We must of spent an hour trying to find the goddamn car. And you say it was here all the time. You didn't maybe move it?"

"Why would I do that, Rocco?"

"That's what I asked myself, Joey. I can't figure it. But hell, it don't matter, I guess. Listen, why don't you come to Jersey with us? You could stay at the house until this thing blows over."

"You forget, Rocco. There's Vickie."

"Yeah. Well, maybe we could drop you someplace?"

Sure, I thought, you could drop me in a Jersey swamp.

"I'd better go alone," I said. "If I get picked up, you wouldn't want to be harboring a fugitive."

"Where you going now, Joey?"

"I'll keep in touch, Rocco."

"Well, good luck."

I shut the door and headed for the elevators at a dead run. I heard the Eldorado start up. The rear tires squealed as Big Augie gunned it. I looked over my shoulder, still running, and saw the big car coming my way. I ducked between two parked cars and crouched there. I had Jock's .38 in my hand. As the Cadillac came up to where I was

crouching, Big Augie slowed it down. His window was open. His left hand was sticking all the way out the window. The gun looked like a Colt .45, which is what he always carried in his shoulder holster. I made myself as small as I could. His gun roared. Mine spoke too, but not as loud. His roared twice, but though I tried for a second shot, it didn't fire. We both missed the kill. Big Augie missed me altogether, but I had caught him in his left arm or hand. I couldn't be sure which. Anyway, he dropped the Colt, stepped on the gas, and got the hell out of there. I stuck the Miroku in its scabbard, picked up Big Augie's Colt and put it in my coat pocket, and got the hell out of there myself.

I didn't wait for an elevator, but took the stairs, running. I slowed down when I reached the first lower level, and was breathing normally by the time I hit ground level, though I was very shaky. It wasn't the first time in my life I'd been under the gun, but you never get used to it.

I called Actor's Chapel from a booth by the Forty-first Street exit, and while Father Vito and I were talking, Vickie's hourly call came through on another line. Vito couldn't switch me over to her, but we managed a three-way conference, with him as intermediary.

She had only one new thing to report: a deadline. The people who were holding her were giving me until midnight to come up with those missing cans of film.

I told Vito to say I was working on it, that I'd already talked to Rocco, that he'd said he didn't have the missing film cans, but that I had certain leads I was going to follow right away and I'd report hourly if possible, on the hour. Vito relayed the message.

Then he told me that someone had hung up Vickie's phone. The gruff-voiced man who'd cut in on my first conversation with Vickie with a threat, had cut in again, saying, *"All* the films, and all copies, or we take the girl apart." Same man, same threat. Vito said Vickie had cried out as she'd done before, seemingly in pain, and they'd hung up.

I asked Vito to call a limousine service and order a car for me. It should be equipped with radio and telephone. And I needed it right away. Taxis are too chancy, too often driven by off-duty cops. Or on-duty cops. Anyway, when are cops ever off duty? Vito asked where I wanted the limo delivered. I told him Actor's Chapel, if he had no objection.

"None at all," he said. "I'd better order it in my name, don't you think?" I said yes, thanked him, and told him I'd be coming directly to the chapel. "And where will you go from here?" he asked. "Where will you start looking for Vickie, or those films, or whatever?"

I said I'd tell him when I got to the chapel.

❦ 9 ❧

WHILE WE WAITED for the limousine, Father Vito and I discussed procedure. He sat at his desk by the windows and I stood by him, watching the back of Pal Joey's, three floors below. It was a bright day and the patio of the club was filled with sunshine. Dogs and cats were enjoying the balmy afternoon in the block's back yards. Pigeons perched on the walls of the gardens. A flock of starlings came swooping in, all talking at once.

The club's kitchen door was open. Two cook's helpers were carrying garbage cans through the patio and out the alleyway to the street. Around the spot where Jock had fallen, a kitchen helper was washing the dried blood away. I saw Dom come out of the kitchen and unlock the cellar door and open it. He would have the helpers store nonperishables like canned and bottled goods below in case of a break-in. After-hours break-ins are very common in our business.

Vito asked where I planned to start my search for

Vickie. I said I thought I'd begin with Mady Prevatte, because with her Park Avenue social standing and her betrothal to an Italian count, she had the most to lose by public exposure of *Pickup on Swing Street*, the film she and Hub Grindel had performed in. They could be holding Vickie for ransom, for their film and the copies of it. They'd have to have help, of course, but with her money she could hire an army, or a gang.

"But Vickie's kidnappers want *all* the films," Vito said, "not just the one Mady and Hub are in."

"Probably a smoke screen," I said. "If they ask for *all* the films, they get the one that matters without revealing who wants it. Whoever burgled Jock's photo studio took *all* the nude stills from the walls, *all* the photo negatives, and *all* the cans of movie film."

"Not all the cans," Vito said. "Apparently some of the movies, or some of the copies, weren't there. They'd already been removed."

"Well, yes," I said.

Vito said, "Maybe none of the films were in the studio when the burglary took place, but certainly the wanted one wasn't there."

"You have a fine Jesuitical mind, Father."

"I think you mean Socratic," Vito said.

"No doubt."

"It has occurred to me," he said, "that those film cans would be labeled."

"Good point. But if the burglar had been instructed to take *all* the cans of movie film, *all* the file of negatives, and *all* the nude stills on the walls, he'd simply take everything without looking at labels. He might not even know which of these things were really wanted. In any case, he apparently didn't get the film or films he wanted or was instructed to take."

Vito said, "If it turns out that Mady can't lead you to Vickie, or to the missing cans of film, who's next on your list?"

"It's a tossup."

"May I make a suggestion?"

"Of course."

"Do you plan to see Chico Grande?"

"If I don't get lucky with Mady."

"Try a shot in the dark," Vito said. "Chico's probably at Sullivan's Gym, training for Saturday's fight. It's only two blocks from here. You could walk in on him, whereas Mady might prove difficult to see. Meanwhile, if you like, I could try to set her up for you. I won't let her know that you've told me about *Pickup on Swing Street.*"

"Right on, Father. And thanks."

"Anything I can do, Joe. We both want to get Vickie."

"Rocco might call you and leave a message for me. I told him about Vickie and the ransom her kidnappers want, all the films and all copies. He said he doesn't have them."

"Do you believe him?" Vito asked.

"I wouldn't take his word for the time of day, Father. When I last saw him, his personal bodyguard, Big Augie Benedetto, was shooting at me with a Colt forty-five."

"For God's sake, Joe! What for?"

"Maybe Rocco doesn't want me mixing into his business. If he's got the missing movies, and the copies, he won't willingly give them up to ransom Vickie, a girl he doesn't know and wouldn't care about on my account. He certainly wouldn't want me trying to get the films away from him. Of course, I don't know that he's got them. But if he has them, he probably figures I'll try and do something. Incidentally, I told him you know nothing about all this, so play it that way if he should get in touch with you. Can you lie, Father?"

"In the cause of truth, yes. But you need police, don't you?"

"I'll want to talk to Sergeant Sweeney when I know a little more. He's the homicide detective who was working on Jock's murder when this Commander Fitzroy took over. Sweeney was trying to be helpful. He didn't believe I killed Jock. He could see I was being framed. He never would have put out a pick-up-and-hold on me, much less a warrant. So I want to talk to him. You know Specks Beamish and Nickels Detroit. I asked them to speak to a friend of theirs on the force, a vice cop, Detective Dan Lee, known as Dan the Man. He could get word to Sweeney. So if Sweeney calls, ask him to leave a safe number where I can call him back."

"Will do," Vito said. "I hate to see you going into this alone. What's your plan, beyond seeing Chico and Mady. What about the others?"

"I'll check them all if I have to."

The doorbell rang, and Vito went downstairs to answer it. Presently he came back, saying it was the limousine. He'd signed for it and told the chauffeur to wait, explaining that one of his parishioners, a Mr. Harold Williams, would be using the car during the afternoon and possibly the evening on parish business.

"It has what you asked for," he said, "telephone and radio. I wrote down the phone number. I'll call you as soon as I have anything to report. There's a glass partition, so the chauffeur can't hear your calls. He's an elderly gentleman and seems to know his job. Very cool and courteous. His name is Andrew."

"Not an off-duty cop?"

"Retired, perhaps," Vito said.

"Even retired, they're never off duty, Father. It's like the priesthood, once and forever."

Vito laughed and said, "It's nearly time for Vickie's call. If you leave now you'll be at Sullivan's Gym when her call comes through."

I checked my watch. Two-fifty. I said I'd wait. He got out a bottle of rosé, which he said his father had made. He poured two small glasses. I offered him a cigar. We lit up and sipped our wine and waited. The rosé was dynamite. It had the delicate taste and aroma of muscat and the kick of a mule.

At precisely three o'clock the phone rang. Vito nodded to me and I picked it up.

"Vickie?"

"Joe?"

"Are you all right?"

"Joe, they've killed him!"

Her voice had that same quavery, almost hysterical tone I'd heard when we talked before. I was about to ask whom they'd killed when she cried out sharply and a man's voice came on the line.

"You got the films, Streeter?"

"Not yet," I said. "I'm working on it. What have you done to Vickie?"

"Nothing much, Streeter. Just a little taste of what she can expect if you don't deliver those films. You talk to Rocco?"

"Yes. He says he hasn't got them. I'm working on another angle."

"Tell me about it."

97

I hoped to tell him about it with a .45-caliber lead slug between the eyes, or maybe in the belly, but I simply said, "Later. I need time. Will you go along?"

"We'll call again at four. Get it on, Streeter. We'll give you until midnight."

"Meanwhile lay off the girl," I said. "You hurt her and I'll hunt you down. I'll kill you nineteen different ways."

He laughed and hung up the phone.

Make it twenty different ways, I thought. One for Schatzi.

⧉ **10** ⧉

ANDREW WAS RUNNING a flannel cloth over the car, a squirrel-gray Bentley, when Father Vito and I came out of the chapel.

Vito said, "Andrew, this is Mr. Harold Williams."

"Very pleased to meet you, sir," said Andrew.

He was about sixty, with gray muttonchop sideburns and a full gray mustache of the Buffalo Bill type, with goatee. He had large milky blue eyes, a bulbous red nose that must have cost him a fortune, and a paunch that looked as if it just might fit behind the wheel. He wore livery of gray twill with brass buttons and a visored cap with a brass emblem: *Elite Limousine Service.*

Vito said, "Andrew, this gentleman will be using the car on parish business, probably all afternoon and possibly this evening too."

"Very good, Father," said Andrew.

He opened the door for me. I thanked Vito, shook his hand, and got into the Bentley. The passengers' windows had Venetian blinds and there were red rosebuds in little silver vases. Radio and telephone, of course. When Andrew was behind the wheel I picked up the speaking tube and told him to take me to Sullivan's Gym on Forty-eighth Street between Eighth and Ninth avenues. He handled the car very smartly.

As we drove west along Forty-ninth I took Jock's little Miroku .38 out of the shoulder holster, cocked it, and examined the firing pin. Old Matt Griffin was right. This piece was junk. The swivel-mounted pin had snapped when I cranked off my second shot at Big Augie. A gun like that could get you killed. But Big Augie's personal Colt .45 was in my coat pocket.

In order to avoid the customary winos and other hooligans hanging around the entrance of the gym, I told Andrew to park across the street. I didn't want those bums sitting on my Bentley and getting it greasy. After all, I expected to be taking Vickie for a ride in it soon.

When Andrew opened my door I told him to open the partition so he could hear the phone. He was to take any calls, ask the caller to hold, then come inside and tell me.

"But lock the car first," I said.

He said yes, sir, and saluted. I told him I didn't expect to be long.

As I came up to the entrance of the gym one of the winos did an elaborate bow and said, "Your lordship!" Another grinned at me and made a sucking sound. I kicked him in the kneecap and went on in, listening contentedly to his howls as I walked down the hallway to the back, where I found Chico Grande working on a sparring partner.

Honey Wing was sitting near the ropes, watching Chico and smiling. She wore a red silk skin-tight dress with no shoulders and nothing below midthigh. A thin black patent-leather belt with a sunburst buckle cinched her small waist, which made one observe that nothing else about her was small. Big breasts, big hips, very shapely legs, fine arms. And her bleached-blond hair was curly and long and looked like it would appear to its best advantage on a bed pillow. Honey didn't notice me coming in. She was too busy watching Chico punch his sparring partner.

The room stank of sweat and cheap cigars and booze. I looked among the groups of men for Chico's owner-manager, Hymie "Doubles" Gross. He was with Honey's producer-procurer, Ruby Porcelain, and some other men at a table with a bottle and glasses, watching the sparring match and talking.

I walked over to Honey. It took her a while to recognize me behind the sunglasses and under the unaccustomed homburg. In another moment Porcelain and Gross got up from their table to come over and see who was talking to Honey. Then Chico backed off from his sparring partner, told him to take five and came over to investigate.

So there we were, Chico Grande and Honey Wing, Ruby Porcelain and Hymie Gross, and me. Of course they knew there was a murder warrant out on me. I could see it in their eyes, even Honey's, a slightly apprehensive, strained, suspicious look as they smiled and we shook hands around. I asked where we could talk, all five of us together, privately. Gross hesitated, then said Sullivan's office. It was a dingy little room with a glass-windowed door. He knocked and asked Sullivan if we could use the place. Jim Sullivan was a big ex-fighter and ex-cop. New York City probably has more ex-cops than any city in the world—in fact, more ex-cops than cops in uniform on duty. Sullivan didn't know me, though I knew him. He'd never been to my club, but I'd often seen him around the Garden on fight nights. When we came in he just grunted and walked out. His crummy little office had sheltered many a quiet deal, a fighter bought, a player sold.

Gross closed the door behind Sullivan and said, "What's up, Joe?"

Porcelain said, "We hear there's a warrant. . . ."

"Yeah," said Gross. "What's it all about, Joe?"

Hymie "Doubles" Gross looked enough like Uncle Rocco Lucarelli to be his brother. A gorilla like Rocco, but Jewish. And being not only Chico Grande's owner-manager but a shylock and a bookie who would on request equalize the laws of chance, he was as much like Rocco as he looked, but without the Family.

"I haven't a lot of time," I said, "so let's get down to business. You all remember Victoria Moorcroft?" They nodded. "She's been snatched," I told them. "Somebody's holding her for ransom. The price is some movies Jock has made. You know about the one called *The Champ*. I want it, and I want the others. I need all of them. So what can you tell me?" The four stood there saying nothing. "Well, come *on!*" I said. "I'm in a hurry. So are the cops. Do you want to talk to me or to them?"

"What's with cops?" Gross said. "There's a warrant. . . ."

"So what have I got to lose?" I asked.

"You want to know what?" asked Gross.

"Have you got the movie Chico and Honey made?"

"No. And we don't know nothing about no others. So what could we tell you?"

I said, "You could start by telling me how come your boy and this girl got into such a movie in the first place."

Gross said, "I don't see how that could help you."

102

"Like chicken soup," I said, "it couldn't hurt."

Gross said, "Chico, tell him."

Chico Grande, a/k/a Canvasback Grande because he spent so much fight time on the canvas, looked like what he was, a punching bag, the nose flat and twisted, the ears knobby like cauliflower, lips puffy, brows heavy like a chimpanzee's, brain loose in the skull.

"Okay, Hymie," said Chico. "See, it's like this, Mr. Streeter, we didn't know each other, Honey and me. I mean, I seen her around, but we never met. So one night at Pal Joey's when me and her was both there, Jock points her out to me and he says, 'Hey, Chico, how you like that?' I say I like it okay. So he says, 'You wanta meet her?' I say sure. So he introduces us, and he invites us up to his studio to see his layout. He says he got some special movies. Okay, so we go up with him. He gives us a drink, and then he breaks out the smoke. Good Colombian grass. Pretty soon he opens up some coke, and we all take one on one, and then two on two. Then he shows us this movie—"

"Which movie was that?" I asked.

"Oh, just one of them loops, like they're called. A guy and a girl making it, you know."

"Recognize the performers?"

"Not the guy, but the girl, yes, one of them topless dancers. I seen her at the Bon Bon Bar. You know the joint?"

"Name?" I asked.

"I don't know her name," Chico said, "but she's a little blond broad, about Honey's build, only her hair's natural. . . ."

"All right," I said. "What happened next?"

"About what?" asked Chico.

"About this film you made, *The Champ.*"

"Oh, yeah. Well, Jock says he's got to go someplace for a while, maybe a couple hours, so why don't we just hang in there and make ourselves comfortable, watch the loops, have a ball, right? Why not? He's got this bar there fulla good booze, and this bowl of Colombian and the little box of real good coke. Man, that coke sparkled like it was diamonds!"

Chico grinned, staring into space, remembering how it was.

"Chico, get it on," I said.

"Right," he said. "We got it on." He put an arm around the short bleached-blond Eurasian, and she looked up at him with onyx eyes inscrutable. She twisted like a cobra dancing to the snake charmer's flute. "Yeah," Chico went on, "we sure did. Only we didn't know Jock was making a movie of us doing it. I guess he must of had a camera stashed out of sight somewheres. We didn't see nothing, but naturally we wasn't looking for no cameras. Anyways, coupla days later Jock calls me up here at the gym and asks me if I want to buy this movie called *The Champ*. He says it's all about me and Honey. He says he'll sell it to me for ten grand. Where would I get ten grand? I tell him I don't want to buy no movie, and he says he could sell it to the movie theaters around town. How do I like that? I don't like it. I'm thinking, it could ruin me as a ring fighter. So I tell him I'll think it over. Then I go and tell Hymie about it."

Gross said, "I told Chico not to worry. It couldn't hurt, right? The odds on this fight are so long nobody bets on the outcome. You're lucky to get a bet on the first two rounds, mostly between early or late in the first. So I figure if Jock makes his threat good, if he sells the movie and it gets around town, it's maybe good for *us*, it could

104

help the gate. Maybe everybody would buy a ticket to see if Canvasback Grande screws the way he fights . . . on his back."

Chico crouched, put up his gloves, and feinted at Gross, grinning. Gross threw a left, Chico caught it.

Gross said, "The only thing is, what if Jock don't show the movie in the theaters like he said. So I tell Chico to make sure, go to Jock at the club, get him mad, tell him to shove the movie up his ass, then lean on him, but hard. That might make sure he showed the movie around. He'd think he was hurting us. So the night he was killed, that's what we was gonna do, lean on him, right in front of the whole damn club. Only somebody got to him first. That's about it, Joe. We never none of us seen this movie he called *The Champ*. We thought about it last night after he was shot and we was talking about it when you come in just now, but the fact is we don't even know for sure he really made this movie. Maybe he was bluffing."

"He wasn't bluffing," I said.

"You seen it?" Chico asked. "How is it? How'd I do?"

"I haven't seen it," I told him. "But I've seen evidence that there is such a film. Jock made several flicks like yours, apparently, involving a number of friends of his." I asked Honey, "What about you? Did Jock offer to sell you a print of *The Champ?*"

"Are you keeding?" she said. "Jock know I don' got no money. He don' even pay me!"

Ruby Porcelain said, "That's right, Joe. The cheap son of a bitch didn't even pay her for performing. He come to me and said he made this movie of Honey and Chico balling, and would I like to buy it for ten thousand dollars or he'd sell it on the street and it'd get shown around the theaters. Hymie and I talked it over. I told Jock, screw it, let him pay Honey for her work. He laughed at me. So I told him at least send us a couple passes so we could see the flick for free."

Ruby Porcelain would rent out his mother. If *The Champ* could increase Chico's gate, it might build Honey's too, right? A big baby-faced "Broadway producer" who couldn't produce a one-acter in Hoboken if you paid him to do it, he lived off women, and currently Honey Wing, refugee pross from Saigon. But she was fine, if you like Oriental dishes.

Well, by now it looked like I had eliminated four suspects, and that was a score. Why would these people kill Jock and kidnap Vickie? They didn't want *The Champ* for themselves, for personal or any other reasons. They only wanted it to be shown publicly because they figured it might help them. If Jock thought he was doing them something dirty, as apparently he did, he was really doing them a big favor.

Gross said, "What about those other movies? Who's in them? Anybody we know?"

Ordinarily that was information I wouldn't feel free to give. But Vickie's life was in danger. Chico and Gross, Honey and Porcelain, didn't know my other film stars personally, but they did know who they were. A long shot, but I played it.

I said, "Mady Prevatte and Hub Grindel, Licia and Lucio Garay, and Athena Hosnani, the Egyptian belly dancer."

Chico said, "Carambas!"

"Mady!" said Honey, laughing. "Oh-ho!" She laughed until she was doubled over, clutching her belly, tears pouring down her cheeks. "Hoo boy!"

Porcelain said, "Why not? These high-society broads

are like all the others. Think she'd work for me, Streeter?"

This half-witty crack sent Honey into another big belly-twisting fit of laughter. Other Oriental women titter and giggle; Honey laughed like a drunken Marine. Maybe she learned to laugh from the leathernecks in Saigon.

Gross said, "What's all this talking around doing for you, Joe?"

"It eliminates four suspects."

"Sure," he said. "Why would any of us want to kill Jock Alfieri?"

"I'm not into Jock's murder right now," I told him. "I'm looking for those *films*. I need them to ransom Vickie."

"Well, *we* ain't got her, and we ain't got the films. I wish we could help you, Joe."

I said, "If you hear anything, call Father Vito at Actor's Chapel. He'll get a message to me."

Chico said, "You find the action, Mr. Streeter, you let me know. I'd like to take care of this guy that snatched your girl."

I said, "Thanks, Chico. Good luck Saturday."

⌘ 11 ⌘

WHEN I HIT THE STREET I found Andrew besieged by half
a dozen bums who'd been hanging around the front of the
gym. They'd gone across the street and were perched like
dirty birds all over the car, sitting on the front fenders and
engine cowling, passing a bottle of wine. Andrew was in
the driver's seat looking scared. He saw me coming and
got out and opened the rear door, but the bums just sat
where they were, grinning drunkenly at me and making
yardbird comments like "Hey, boys, here comes Chaun-
cey! Give the gentleman room, you bums!" The combination of a classy Bentley with a man dressed like I was,
homburg, chesterfield, dark glasses, and in this neighborhood, Ninth Avenue and Forty-eighth Street, the edge of
Hell's Kitchen, was to say the least a natural target. So I
thought I'd fraternize and relieve the pressure. I approached the bum who held the wine bottle and asked
him for a drink. He got off the fender where he sat. Nothing for nothing, he said, and I fished some coins out of my

pants pocket and put a few quarters in his greasy palm. He handed me the bottle. I took a long pull at it, filling my mouth with the sickly sweet stuff, blew it in his face, tossed the bottle into a nearby trash basket, pulled the other bums off the car and flung them helter-skelter into the street. Then I got into the car, Andrew closed my door and got in front, and we both locked our doors. The bums picked themselves off the asphalt and began beating on the windows, howling and cursing. One of them retrieved the bottle from the trash basket. Another pulled a long kitchen knife and started hacking at a front tire. Andrew started the motor, and I told him to put it in first gear and dig out of there like a drag racer. He did, sending the bums flying all over the street. Just a little quiet fun on a Hell's Kitchen afternoon. I'm sure we all felt better for it.

"There were no calls," Andrew said over the intercom. "Where to now, sir?"

"Head for Fifty-ninth Street," I told him. "Take a turn in the park, the long way around."

He hung a left at Eighth Avenue. My wrist watch said five to four, so I phoned Actor's Chapel, hoping Father Vito had heard from Sergeant Sweeney. He hadn't. But he'd talked to Mady Prevatte, and she was willing to see me. She was expecting me at her pied-à-terre in the Sherry-Netherland. He'd explained to her that I was using the name of Harold Williams, which he'd done in case she was worried about the murder warrant that was out for Joseph Streeter.

I told Vito about the interview at Sullivan's Gym. He agreed that at least I'd probably eliminated four suspects. This left Mady Prevatte and Hub Grindel, the Garay twins, and Athena Hosnani.

Vito said he wasn't sure about the Garays or Athena, but

he felt confident about Mady. She wouldn't want a porno-graphic film about her shown in Times Square movie houses. She'd certainly pay blackmail. After all, someone had given Jock that ten thousand dollars and of all the suspects, she was the most likely. She'd probably do just about anything to kill the film of her and Hub Grindel if she'd been tricked into performing for Jock's hidden cam-era. . . .

But we got no further, for Vickie's call came through then. We handled it the way we did her previous call, with Vito acting as intermediary, but this time they didn't let her speak on the phone. Instead it was the gruff-voiced man who'd made the threat to "take the broad apart." He asked what was happening, and I told Vito to tell him I wouldn't talk to anyone but Vickie.

When Vito had relayed the message and got an an-swer, he said the man claimed Vickie couldn't come to the phone. I demanded to know why. Because, he said, she wasn't feeling well. And he said I should "shut up about the broad and talk business." So I said all right, I was working on his problem for him and I'd already eliminated four persons who'd been involved in Jock's movies—

The man interrupted Vito's report to ask what I meant by "eliminated." I told Vito to tell him to figure it out for himself. I added that I was then on my way to check out another suspect. Vito relayed this bit, and the man asked who the suspect was. I told Vito to ignore the question and to give the man my car phone number, tell him I'd expect his next call at five, remind him that kidnapping is a fed-eral crime and I'd go to the FBI if Vickie didn't make the next call herself, personally.

The man gave Vito a lot of static about the murder

110

warrant that was out on me, and I told Vito to tell him to stow it. And that was that. The man hung up.

I told Vito not to give the car phone number to Sergeant Sweeney if he should call, but to ask him for a safe number where I could call him.

The Bentley had nearly completed the long turn around Central Park. I told Andrew to take me to the Sherry-Netherland. It was a great day for romping in the park with Schatzi. She was an expert Frisbee catcher. I'd throw it and she'd chase it, wait under it, then leap up and snatch it in flight. Then she'd bring it back to me, grinning and wagging her tail.

❧ 12 ☙

THE SHERRY-NETHERLAND IS ON FIFTH AVENUE just north of the plaza and is one of Manhattan's most exclusive apartment hotels. Having a mere walk-in flat, a pied-à-terre, at this hostelry is just about as ostentatious as a Texas oil heiress can get, especially when she also has a townhouse two blocks away on Park Avenue. We pulled up in front, and I told Andrew to park nearby and wait. If a call came through he should ask the caller to hold, then go to the desk in the lobby and ask for me in Miss Prevatte's apartment. He got out and opened my door. The hotel doorman was right there with dollar signs tattooed on his eyeballs. I gave him a five and he pointed Andrew to a spot he'd been saving, just two cars up the block. Andrew backed and parked.

I went into the elegant lobby, told the desk clerk I was Mr. Harold Williams, and said Miss Prevatte was expecting me.

"Yes, Mr. Williams," he said. "The bellman will take you up."

He summoned a bellboy, who looked like a retired jockey who'd ridden a lot of losers. He was skinny, wrinkled, and tired. He took me up to a penthouse apartment and waited with me while I pushed the buzzer. I gave him a dollar. He muttered something. When a maid opened the door and I'd said I was Harold Williams, the bellhop went back to the elevator. He hadn't thanked me for the dollar.

I followed the maid into a foyer, where she left me. The foyer was bigger than many New Yorkers' apartments and much fancier. Wall-to-wall white shag carpet, a huge walk-in closet for guests' coats and hats, Louis XV divans, ornate gilt-framed Barbizon originals on two walls, French and Italian fashion magazines on nacre-inlaid mahogany coffee tables.

Mady sashayed in, doing her Mae West walk, and said, "How come the Harold Williams bit, sweetie?" A rhetorical question, so I let it ride and just said hello. She was wearing a tailored pants suit of silver silk lamé. Her hair was ash blond today. I'd seen it red, black, and mauve on various occasions, so I had no idea what it really was. Maybe mouse gray. "I heard about the murder warrant," she said. "You on the lam, sweetie? Care for a drink?" Her Texas accent was a bit thicker than usual. "Hang your coat and hat in the closet there," she said. "You look real weird in those sunglasses."

I hung up the coat and hat and put the glasses in my pocket. Big Augie's gun was in the coat. My back was to Mady as I hung the coat, so I slipped the gun out of it and stuck it in my belt, way over on the left, and buttoned the jacket. A Colt .45 tends to make a bulge that way, but the bulge itself can be a deterrent to some people. Jock's little Miroku .38 was still in its shoulder holster and as useless as the teats on a boar, as they say in Texas, so I needed the Colt where I could reach it quick.

My first impulse when the Miroku misfired had been to throw it in the nearest trash basket, but my second thought had been to keep it. Maybe eventually it could tell me something. I might have Sergeant Sweeney check out the ballistics. Anyway, it didn't cost me anything to keep it.

"I have to ask you a few questions, Mady," I said.

"I don't know anything about Jock's murder," she said.

"It's about some movies Jock made," I said.

"I need a drink," she said. "Come on in."

I followed her into the parlor, a thirty-by-forty salon with a parquet floor, Aubusson carpets, Steinway concert grand, red leather couches, overstuffed chairs, and windows overlooking Central Park.

Mady Prevatte's resemblance to a young Mae West wasn't coincidental. She'd cultivated it, including the walk and the talk, especially when she was blond. She was a little on the heavy side, like Miss West, though taller than the actress. She had the West cool, the poise, the sang-froid.

"Make mine cognac," I said.

She said, "Would you take care of it, sweetie? I'm a little nervous. Too much bubbly today. I think I'd better switch to bourbon. On the rocks, no water."

I set them up on the half-moon bar, bourbon for her, cognac for me. She was leaning on the Steinway, watching me. The bubbly she'd been drinking was Roederer's Cristal. A nearly empty magnum stood in an ice bucket and there were two champagne glasses on the bar.

I gave her the bourbon and she took a long pull at it. Her hands had a slight tremor. I sipped my cognac and waited.

She took a deep breath and said, "What about these movies you mentioned?"

I said, *"Pickup on Swing Street,* starring Mady Prevatte and Hub Grindel . . ."

I let it go at that. She turned away from me and went to the windows. I set my drink on a coffee table, sat down to the Steinway, and played the intro to "High Society." She was looking out the windows at the park. I don't know if she saw what she was looking at. I got into the Picou riff. She didn't seem to hear. I waited.

Presently she turned back to me. I stopped playing and stood up.

She said, "How do you know about our picture?"

I said, "I know about all of Jock's movies."

"All?"

"All. He was trying to blackmail certain persons besides you."

She smiled now as if she'd just devoured a canary. She all but licked the feathers off her chops.

"Sweetie, have I got news for you! Jock wasn't blackmailing me. I *paid* him to make that movie."

I knocked back the rest of my cognac.

"You *paid* Jock to make a pornographic movie of you and Hub Grindel?"

"Um-hum."

"I don't believe you."

"Take it or leave it, sweetie."

"Why would you pay anyone to make such a film?"

"You'd never understand, sweetie."

"Try me."

"Call it a *souvenir d'amour*."

"A remembrance of love? I don't get it, Mady."

"I'm engaged to be married, darling. It's what the French call a *mariage de convenance*. I'm marrying an Italian count. Not a love match, but Count Carlo is satisfactory in other ways. And I'll be a countess. I'm sure it must seem silly to you, dear, but it doesn't to me. You see, Hub and I have had a perfectly marvelous relationship, and we both hate to see it end. We've been very good lovers for a very long time. So since we'll miss one another, I thought of a way to keep the memory of it alive when I'm nothing but an old countess a few years from now and he's playing mature roles in Hollywood. We're both crowding forty, you see. . . ."

I said, "Mady, you're crazy."

She laughed and turned toward an open doorway and called, "Hub, darling! Come on in here."

Hub Grindel came striding into the parlor, relaxed and smiling.

"How are you, Joe?" he said. He offered his hand. I shook it. He was a handsome man in a pretty sort of way. "I couldn't help hearing," he said. "What Mady told you is the plain truth. We've been together a long time, Joe, since school days in Dallas when we both got held back and had to repeat the eighth grade before they'd let us graduate."

Mady said, "God's honest truth, Joe. We spent so much time in my grandfather's hayloft we didn't get any studying done. After junior high, Grandpa sent me away to a girls' school in Vermont, and Hub ran away from home to be near me."

I said, "How come you two never married? Or did you?"

"What for?" Mady said. "What could marriage give us that we didn't have already?"

"But you're marrying this Italian count."

"It's the title, sweetie. Does that seem just awful to you?"

"Matter of fact," I said, "it does. It also seems to make you vulnerable to blackmail."

"I told you, darling, Jock wasn't blackmailing us."

"Did he give you *all* the prints of your movie?"

"No. He was *supposed* to give us two copies last night, but before he could . . ."

"All right," I said. "But where does this leave Hub? After all these years together, you buy yourself an Italian count, leaving Hub out in the cold."

Hub said, "It's not like that, Joe. We'll see each other from time to time. I'm going out to the Coast in a few days. Finally got my break. I'll be working in television, a new series, a good role. And Mady's going off to Europe to be married. But we'll always see each other when we can."

I thought of my own relationship with Vickie. Not so different from Mady's and Hub's, after all.

I said, "But what if your movie, or a copy of it, a print, happened to fall into the wrong hands?"

"We thought of that," Hub said. "Too late. We've been talking it over today. Jock's getting killed last night could bring bad trouble. We didn't know he'd made other films like ours. A lot of people *could* be in trouble."

"What about this film?" I said. *"Pickup on Swing Street* — what's the significance of the title? Why give it a title at all, if it was just a *souvenir d'amour,* as you say?"

"Oh, the title was Jock's idea," Mady said. "What we wanted, Hub and I, was a film showing us doing the things we usually do, like meeting at a spot, you know, having a few drinks, taking a walk, going for a buggy ride in Central Park, then coming back here, getting it on. . . ."

"I'm puzzled," I said. "I can see you performing for Jock's camera in scenes like having drinks in a bar, taking a stroll up the avenue, going for a ride in the park, but the bedroom bit—wasn't Jock watching while you and Hub . . . ?"

"Heavens, no!"

"Just asking, Mady."

"You don't think we're exhibitionists, do you? Jock set up his camera, started the film rolling, and left us alone. Sweetie, you've got a dirty mind."

"Sorry."

I could see it now. Same situation as Chico's and Honey's except that when Jock photographed them he'd used a hidden camera and when he photographed Mady and Hub he didn't have to hide it. He only had to leave the room. I wondered if he'd peeked. I thought he probably had. My ex-partner and ex-buddy was coming up full of surprises.

Mady said, "What's *your* interest in all this, Joe? You surely don't think *we* killed Jock? Or was dear Jocko blackmailing *you?* An old stud like you performing in a sex movie?"

I said, "Certain people are trying to get hold of the films Jock made, all copies of all the films, and I'm the one who has to get it together."

"Why you?"

"They've kidnapped Vickie."

118

"*Your* Vickie?"

"Yes."

"Who *are* these people?"

"I don't know. But I'm trying to find out. They say her ransom is all the films Jock made, all copies, all prints. Or they'll take her apart, as they put it. They've given me until midnight. I've talked to them on the phone. I've also talked to Vickie on the phone and it's true, all right. She's in real danger and she says they've already killed somebody in this caper."

"Somebody besides Jock?"

"Yes. I don't know who. But the last time I talked with Vickie on the phone, she said they'd killed somebody. I'm sure she didn't mean Jock."

"You're saying she was free to talk?"

"Not exactly free. There was somebody with her."

Hub said, "Maybe she was told to say that?"

"Maybe."

"They think you have the films?"

"No. They think—or they thought—Jock's uncle, Rocco Lucarelli, has them. They told me to talk to Uncle Rocco, and I did, but he says he doesn't have them. So I'm trying to locate them by going directly to the people involved in them."

"Why didn't the kidnappers talk to Rocco themselves?"

"I don't know. Maybe they couldn't get to him. I can, and they must have known that."

"But how come they want *all* the films? Does that mean ours too?"

"I think they're asking for all the films because they don't want to single out the one film they really want."

"How do *you* know who's in Jock's films? How did you know about *us?*"

"I can't divulge that," I said. I didn't know why I said it. Maybe because Hub and Mady were asking a lot of questions and I was just naturally clamming up. I said, "Sorry."

"If you could figure out which film they really want," Hub said, "you'd know who's holding Vickie for ransom, wouldn't you?"

"That's the idea," I said. "So far I've eliminated two films and six suspects. That leaves two more films and three suspects."

Hub said, "Mind telling us who?"

"First," I said, "I'd like to take a look around the apartment."

Mady said, "You don't think *we* have Vickie?"

"No, Mady, but I'd like to take a look."

Hub said, "Now, see here . . . !"

But Mady said, "Let him look, dear."

I went through it, all six rooms. I hadn't really expected to find her or any trace of her. Mady and Hub were not the kind of people who commit murder or kidnapping. Kooks, yes, but not crazy. They wouldn't even hurt a dog.

They'd waited for me in the parlor, and when I came back I told them the rest of it: "The Garay twins did their 'Kama Sutra Tango' for Jock, apparently in the nude, performing the *Kama Sutra* positions they usually do in costume in their dance. And Athena Hosnani did her belly dance in the nude. It's a short called *Danse du Ventre.*"

Hub said, "How did Jock get them to perform? Did he pay them, or what? I can't imagine anyone else doing what Mady and I did—you know, hiring Jock as a cinematographer."

I said, "I don't know all of it, but he made a film called *The Champ*, with Chico Grande and Honey Wing. He

120

mousetrapped them, used a hidden camera. I thought that was how he photographed you two. I think he might have done that with the Garays. But Athena, no. I've seen a nude still of her that he kept in his wallet. When she posed for that shot, she knew what she was doing. Take my word for it. She knowingly performed her belly dance for Jock's camera and did it willingly in the nude. I don't know why. Maybe they were having an affair."

Mady said, "If Athena posed willingly, that lets her out, doesn't it? She couldn't be involved in Jock's murder or Vickie's kidnapping." I nodded. "And if he did the twins the way he did Chico and Honey, that lets them out too, doesn't it? He could be arrested for extortion."

"I'll have to check out the Garays, but I believe you're right about Athena. And I still think the twins might be blackmailable. How much did you pay Jock to make your film?"

"Ten thousand dollars," Mady said.

"Cash?"

"Used twenties and tens. Jock said he didn't want to see Internal Revenue get any of it."

"The cops got it," I said. "Last night after the murder they tossed the whole building. They found the money in an empty film can in Jock's darkroom. Naturally it looked like blackmail. And I learned he was trying to sell *The Champ* to Chico and Honey. So even though the ten grand was a legitimate fee for services, Jock was definitely into blackmail. He could easily have made extra prints of *Pickup on Swing Street.*"

"Well, as it is," Mady said, "he didn't even deliver the two I paid for. He was supposed to, last night, as I told you, but . . . My God! Who's got them? Joe! You've *got* to find them! This is awful! Think what could happen!"

"I'm thinking about it," I said.

She was worried about going public. Whoever had her movie could blackmail her with it. If she refused to pay, it could be sold. Her debut as an actress would be sensational.

"Joe, listen, you've got to get that film," she said. "I'll pay you. Name it. But get that—"

"I'm trying," I said. "I don't need your money, sweetie. I just need Vickie. It looks like I'll have to find those films in order to ransom her. When I do, I'll turn yours over to you. All copies."

"How can I help?"

It was nearly five o'clock and time for Vickie's hourly call. I had to find out from the gruff-voiced man whether she was unharmed. He hadn't let me speak to her during the four-o'clock call. I didn't think he would now. But I meant to try.

I asked Mady if I could use her phone and would it be all right if I received a call within the next few minutes. She said of course, anything I wanted. I phoned the Bentley and told Andrew that there'd be a call at five o'clock or a minute after. He should tell the caller to phone me at Miss Prevatte's apartment, and I gave him the number.

By five after five I hadn't received the call, so I tried Father Vito. He said the gruff-voiced man had phoned and said to tell me not to try any more stupid tricks. He would call Father Vito's number again at six. And no other number.

Vito had asked him to put Vickie on the line so he could report to me if she sounded all right. Vickie had then come on, saying, "Father Vito? They tell me you want to know if I'm all right. I'm not. . . ."

Someone had hung up her phone then with a crash, but

122

not before Vickie screamed.

Pain, I thought. Or terror. A scream means one or the other. Possibly both. I didn't believe they'd kill her. They couldn't trade a corpse for the films they wanted, and they couldn't know how the exchange would be set up. No doubt they'd try to set it up their way, but they couldn't be sure I'd go along. So Vickie would be alive. Hurt, no doubt, but alive. Until midnight.

I asked Vito if he knew Lieutenant Michael Maginnis well enough to recognize his voice over the phone.

"I think so," Vito said. "As you know, he often comes to mass at the chapel and we've met socially, at your place and elsewhere. Why?"

"How would you describe his voice, Father?"

"Very Irish, tight, high-pitched, almost shrill, an Irish tenor without the brogue."

I said, "I was thinking about the gruff-voiced man on the phone."

"I see," Vito said. "Well . . . No, I don't think so, Joe. The man on the phone has a harsh, rough-edged voice. Mike's is smooth. Why do you ask?"

"I'm sure Maginnis set Jock up for the kill, and there are two people I haven't cleared—the Garay twins. If the Garays killed Jock, then Maginnis could have been the man on the phone with Vickie. But if the voices don't match, that blows hell out of my theory."

Vito said, "If you'll heed the advice of a Jesuit, carefully trained in logic, lay off the theorizing, Joe. Go after the facts. It's okay to check out the Garays, but I don't believe the twins are capable of all this—a murder, burglary, kidnapping. But check them out."

Either one of the Garays could have been the killer I'd seen in the patio of the club, with false rat's-tail mustache, false goatee, and false sideburns. Now that I thought it over, Lucio Garay wouldn't have had to use false hair and gum arabic for the sideburns. He had real ones.

But how could either of the Garays get to the set of keys we kept in the office safe? For they'd have to get those keys in order to enter my apartment and take my P-38, and to enter Jock's photo studio.

Father Vito didn't believe it, and I didn't really believe it myself, but the Garays did seem possible suspects now that I'd eliminated Chico and Honey, and Mady and Hub. The twins *could* have murdered Jock. And not having got the film of their nude "Kama Sutra Tango," they'd still be trying to get it. They'd demand all of Jock's movies and all copies in order not to reveal their identity; also in order not to throw suspicion on themselves as Jock's killers.

But one detail hung me up. That gruff voice I'd heard on the telephone during Vickie's calls couldn't be Lucio's and certainly not his sister Licia's. And so I'd thought of Maginnis, who'd been on the scene, who'd probably set Jock up, and who'd ducked out when the hit went down. But I didn't think he knew the Garays at all. I wasn't sure he'd even seen them dance at the club.

If I had to think in order to play the piano, I'd be better off with a hayfork. Theory. Vito was right. Get the facts. Belay all this theorizing. Trying to have the kidnappers' call relayed to Mady's apartment wasn't smart. Very poor thinking. I needed help.

I told Vito, "It *has* to be the Garays. I've eliminated everyone else."

"Including the Hosnani woman?" Vito asked.

"Yes," I said. "I'm sure she performed willingly."

"So she wouldn't be blackmailable?"

"Right, Father, and that leaves *only* the Garays."

"Well, it's logical," Vito said. "But logic has led saints into error, Joe. Beware of logic. Look to your basic premise."

When I hung up the phone Mady said, "Was that Father Vito you were talking to?"

I said, "It was. He's trying to help."

"Then he knows about Hub and me, the film we made?"

"He does."

"You bastard!"

Hub said, "I ought to whip you like a dog, you son of a bitch!"

"Don't sweat it," I told them. "All you've got to do is go to Father and confess. He'll absolve you."

Mady said, "Joe, you're rotten."

"Sorry if I embarrassed you," I said. "But I can't be fussy when it comes to getting Vickie away from her kidnappers. Father Vito is being very helpful. I need an anchor man, and he's hanging in there by the phone."

"I spoke hastily," Mady said. "I hope you find Vickie all right. *And* get those films . . ."

I said, "Somebody killed my dog."

"Schatzi?"

"Shot between the eyes by whoever burgled Jock's photo studio last night."

"Who would do a rotten thing like that? She was such a sweet dog," Mady said.

❧ 13 ❧

ANDREW SAID the call I'd mentioned hadn't come through, but of course I knew that. I don't know why I thought it would. Thinking again! Some people never learn.

Jock's card index gave a Christopher Street address and phone number for the Garay twins. I told Andrew to take Fifty-ninth over to Seventh Avenue and then down to the Village, and I called them on the car phone. No answer. I knew where their agent-manager-impresario lived but not his phone, so I tried Information, got the number, called it. When he answered, I hung up. It was enough to know he was home. I didn't want to interrogate him by phone, and I didn't need an appointment to see him.

We were still moving west on Fifty-ninth Street and had come to Seventh Avenue, so I gave Andrew the new direction and he turned down the avenue and took a left on Fifty-sixth Street. Just as we pulled up in front of Valentino's apartment the car phone's light flashed and a tiny

126

bell rang. It was Father Vito.

He said, "I've heard from Specks just now. He gave me a message from a Mr. Tramontana, manager of the Bon Bon Bar. This Mr. Tramontana wants to talk to you."

"Thanks, Father."

"Would it have anything to do with Vickie?"

"No idea. I'll call Tramontana right away. Thanks again."

I got Information and the number of the Bon Bon Bar, the topless joint on Eighth Avenue where Marie La Touche, Judy Piper, and Olga Herasimchuk performed. I knew Phil Tramontana only slightly. Jock had introduced us one afternoon when we'd been bumming around. I figured Tramontana probably knew more about me than I knew about him. I thought that in the circumstances his call might have something to do with my problem, though I couldn't imagine how. I called the Bon Bon. He answered and I identified myself.

He said, "Glad you called, Mr. Streeter. I have to talk to you about an important matter. It may be of considerable interest to you."

"What's it about, Mr. Tramontana?"

"Please, not on the phone."

"Where then?"

"You tell me."

"I'll call you back. I'm very busy right now."

"When may I expect your call, Mr. Streeter?"

"I don't know, but as soon as I can make it."

"The sooner the better, sir. We ought to be meeting *now*. Immediately."

"How long will you be at the Bon Bon?"

"Until I hear from you."

"Hang in there. I'll get back to you."

"Soon, Mr. Streeter!"

I hung up and told Andrew to take a message if the phone rang and to wait unless a patrol told him to move, then he should circle the block until I came out.

Candy Valentino's apartment was in a narrow four-story building. There were two small apartments on each floor, small but expensive. The building was situated between Orsini's and the Champignon, two of the best restaurants still surviving in Manhattan. The really good ones died of inflation. I used to visit a girl named Dianne (with two *n*'s) in Valentino's building some years ago. This was before she split for the contrary coast. Why do they always split? This was also before Candy Valentino came up from Miami, before the Cuban Revolution ran the pimps and dealers and other businessmen out of Havana.

The register in the foyer listed *C. Valentino, 1–A.* I rang. Presently a gravelly voice on the intercom said something unintelligible. It was an old intercom and made a rusty sound.

I said, "It's Joe Streeter."

The voice said, "I'm busy."

It said something else I couldn't make out. But I was sure it was Valentino's voice.

I said, "It's important, Candy."

"Busy," the intercom rasped. "Can't see you now. Call me in a couple hours."

The intercom went dead. I had to wait on *him?* I rang the bell again, a long ring. He came back on.

"Yes?"

"We talk *now,*" I told him. "Or I go and bring the cops."

I heard the buzzer, pushed the door open, and walked into the hall. His apartment was the first on the right. He was standing in the doorway.

"What's this about cops, Streeter?"

"That's not what it's about," I said. "It's about a movie your clients made."

"Come inside," he said.

These one-room apartments cost five bills a month, unfurnished. Valentino had decorated his himself: pink satin couch, tubular chrome chairs with red plastic seats and backs, a *Playboy* calendar on a wall, hand-painted landscapes of prerevolutionary Cuba, a Virgin with a red votive light (electric) in a corner.

Licia and Lucio Garay were sitting close together on the pink satin couch, looking as alike as brother-and-sister twins can look, almost identical. They must have heard my dialogue with Valentino on the intercom. They looked scared. I greeted them, and Lucio got up and offered his hand. I shook it. Licia offered me hers. I bowed low over it and kissed it. There was no one else in the apartment, just Candy Valentino, the Garays, and me.

Logic had sent me here, but as Father Vito had said, logic has led saints into error.

Candido Valentino was a man of parts. Everything he touched turned to money, but his economic base was cocaine. He dealt to theater people, musicians, and high society. None of your ten-dollar bags. Nothing less than hundred-dollar spoons, and mostly larger quantities, from quarter ounces on up. He'd handle pounds or kilos if the bread was right. He invested his coke money where he thought it would make a profit—a discotheque on the East Side, a gay bar in Greenwich Village, a cathouse on Murray Hill, a small recording company midtown, a rock group, and currently the Garay twins. He'd first seen them performing at my club and immediately put them under contract. If nothing went wrong, he'd get them

129

into the Empire Room at the Waldorf, then television, tours, Europe. . . .

Candy the Dandy was short, very fat, sleek—a brown-skinned Cuban mestizo with tiny black eyes encased in rolls of fat, a pencil-thin mustache, long black sideburns, black hair carefully waved, and nostrils like twin wind tunnels, for he was a heavy user of his own high-quality candy. He dressed as sharply as a fat man can, everything tailored, and he wore enough jewels on his fingers and wrists to get himself killed if he ever walked alone at night unarmed. I've known only one man who wore as much jewelry as Candy the Dandy and that was Gentleman John Volos.

I looked at the twins, sitting cheek by cheek on the pink satin. They flashed quick bright smiles at me but said nothing. They never said much anyway, except perhaps to each other when they were alone. Maybe not then either. Maybe such close twins communicate by telepathy. Certainly their English wasn't very communicative, being the sort of pidgin you hear in the cantinas of Miami when a gringo wanders in and the locals start sounding on him. But I've worked in clubs all over Latin America and can make myself understood, so we spoke Spanish.

I said, "Vickie's been kidnapped."

That did it. I had their attention. I told them the whole story, beginning with Jock's murder and ending with Vickie's kidnapping.

"The ransom is *all* the films Jock made, and all copies," I said.

"Movies?" Candy said. "Plural?"

I said, "He made five that I know of, including *The Kama Sutra Tango.*"

"You talked with the people in the other movies?"

"All but one," I said. "I guess I'll have to talk to her next. But while I'm here I'd like to know why Licia and Lucio performed in the nude for Jock's movie camera. Was it entrapment?"

Lucio said, "Was it what?"

"Did he trick you and your sister into doing it?"

"No," Lucio said. "We agreed to do it."

Licia smiled and nodded agreement.

Candy said, "Jock tricked us, all right. He said the film would be released only to high-class art theaters. Then he tried to blackmail us. He said if we didn't buy the film from him he'd sell it to the hard-core porno syndicate."

"And it *isn't* hard-core?"

"No, man. The kids did their regular act, but in the nude, that's all. No hard-core porn, not porn at all, no screwing, just dancing the tango naked. Of course they sort of make a pass at the *Kama Sutra* positions in the dance, but no actual balling. This movie could have won at Cannes. But that Jock Alfieri, that cheap . . . !"

"Then there's nothing in *The Kama Sutra Tango* he could use to blackmail you?"

"I wouldn't say that, Joe. He did try to sell us the film under the threat of peddling it on the porn market."

I said, "Well, I've *got* to find the films. That's the ransom. Do you know anything, any of you?"

Candy said, "Who's in the other movies?"

I said, "Chico Grande and Honey Wing, Mady Prevatte and Hub Grindel, and Athena Hosnani. Ring any bells?"

"You say you checked them out, all but one?"

"All but Athena."

"I'd ring *that* bell, Joe."

✌ 14 ✍

THE BENTLEY WAS GONE when I came out. A patrol must have told Andrew to move it. That's democracy. The cops roust not only Chevies and Fords, but Bentleys and Rolls-Royces. While I waited for Andrew to return I took another fling at thinking. Logically Candy Valentino was right. My only remaining suspect was Athena Hosnani, assuming my basic premise that someone involved in Jock's porn movies was involved in Jock's murder and/or Vickie's kidnapping.

But was Athena's *Danse du Ventre* pornography? *The Kama Sutra Tango* wasn't, according to Valentino and the Garays. So if the kidnappers were trying to retrieve one particular movie (by demanding all of them), was it a porn film they were after? Else why bother? And how pornographic could *Danse du Ventre* be—a belly dancer doing her thing, but in the nude. . . . Certainly it couldn't be hard-core. Well, on second thought, yes, it could be. Not a pretty thought.

I saw the Bentley rounding the corner of Sixth Avenue, and when it rolled up to the curb I told Andrew to stay put and I got in. He said there'd been a phone call from Father Vito. I returned the call.

Vito asked if I'd heard the news. It was on the radio just now: another Lucarelli business had been hit. Some gunmen had shot but not killed David Bernstein, manager of Tulipano Wines and Liquors, a Madison Avenue importer and wholesale dealer. I knew Dave Bernstein as I'd known Milt Cohen, the manager of Petrocelli Products, the meat-packaging firm in Chelsea that had been hit early this morning. We bought supplies from both firms for Pal Joey's. I asked Father Vito how he knew Tulipano Wines and Liquors was a Lucarelli enterprise.

"The police have uncovered the Lucarelli interest in all three places," he said. "Your club, Petrocelli Products, and Tulipano Wines and Liquors. They're looking for Rocco. They want to question him. What do you make of that, Joe?"

"I'm thinking," I said. "At least I think so. The Lucarelli connection, right? Jock Alfieri, nominal manager and co-owner of Pal Joey's, then Milt Cohen, actual manager and co-owner of Petrocelli Products, and now Dave Bernstein, actual manager and co-owner of Tulipano Wines and Liquors. Six factors, two pairs of owners for each of three places. Uncle Rocco, the common denominator. How am I doing, Father?"

"Fine," Vito said. "You've just retied the Gordian Knot."

"Can you cut it?"

"I'm wondering if there's more than one common denominator. The managers . . . ?"

"No," I said. "Jock wasn't our actual manager. Dom

133

Ambrosini, the maitre d', is the real manager. Uncle Rocco told me so when we talked at the Plaza last night. Jock wasn't killed because he was the manager of Pal Joey's. He wasn't even co-owner except on the books. Rocco was."

"Unless," Vito said, "the killer didn't know Jock wasn't the actual manager. Or co-owner."

"This isn't cutting it, Father. Anyhow, my problem isn't who killed Jock; it's who's got Vickie."

"Afraid my fine Socratic mind isn't helping much, Joe. You're right, though. The problem *is* finding Vickie, not Jock's killer—unless the killer and the kidnapper are the same . . . ?"

I said, "Father, when you get the next call from Vickie, listen carefully to the man with the gruff voice, the guy who threatens to take Vickie apart. Listen carefully for characteristics like tone, cadence, regional accent, even foreign accent. I thought I heard something when I talked to him, but I'm not sure. You've talked to him since."

"I didn't notice anything unusual," Vito said. "But I'll listen more carefully when he calls again. You have a point to make, Joe?"

"Think Greek."

"Yes," Vito said. "Are you going to try the Hosnani woman next?"

"No, I'm going to try a hunch."

"Good luck. Call me on the hour."

⊰ 15 ⊱

I TOLD ANDREW to drop me in front of the Bon Bon Bar, between Forty-second and Forty-third streets on Eighth Avenue, then circle the block until I came out. I didn't want to subject him to the abuse he would probably have to take from the hustlers in that block, the pimps, midnight cowboys, drag queens, vice cops. A chauffeured Bentley in this block was just asking for it.

The bouncer at the door of the Bon Bon seemed to think I didn't belong, for he blocked the doorway as I came up to it.

"Full house, Mac," he said. "Try around the corner."

"Tell Tramontana I'm here," I said.

"Okay," he said. "Who do I say?"

"You don't."

This bouncer was right for the job—outsize like Big Augie, solid, tough. He looked me up and down and decided it was Tramontana's problem. The homburg, the chesterfield coat, and the dark glasses must have done it.

135

He'd seen the costume before.

"I'll tell him," he said. "Come inside."

He left me at the bar, which was lined with losers sitting cheek by jowl and staring without expression at the topless girls. A juke was blaring rock. The bar was horseshoe-shaped, with a raised runway going down the middle where the girls did whatever they do, which you couldn't call dancing. They moved to the beat, but only to show naked flesh as provocatively and enticingly as they knew how. Crude. Raunchy. They could only provoke and entice the stony-faced losers. There were ordinarily three girls on the runway, but at the moment there were only two: Marie La Touche and Judy Piper. The third girl, Olga Herasimchuk, was waiting table. Fully dressed. Maybe she'd caught cold. As Marie and Judy performed, they caressed themselves lasciviously, fondling their breasts, rubbing their bellies, fingering their belly buttons, feeling their crotches, and pulling aside the G-strings to reveal pubic hair and vulvae. They smiled at the losers all the while, smiles that would freeze your blood. The losers didn't watch the smiles, and they didn't watch the eyes. This inattention has been known to get johns ripped off, even killed. Always watch a hooker's eyes. You may see murder.

The girls saw me come in, but at first didn't recognize me in my costume. But then they did, all three of them, and their fixed smiles faded. By now everybody who knew me also knew there was a warrant out. I was a leper.

The bouncer came back with Phil Tramontana, who took me to his office in the rear of the joint. He had a dirty little room with a greasy window giving on a dim light well. He sat in a swivel chair at his desk, and I sat on a stool. He came to the point.

136

"These raids on Rocco's places," he said. "What do you think, Mr. Streeter?"

I said, "Why do you ask?"

"Because it all started at your club," he said. "So I thought you might know something I don't. I'm worried about the Bon Bon. Maybe it could happen here."

Philip Tramontana was giving out free information. Uncle Rocco was a co-owner, if not outright owner, of this topless joint.

I said, "Why here?"

He said it all: "Three of Rocco's managers get shot. Who's next? Maybe me, right? I want to know what's going on!"

I said, "So do I. But none of the topless bars have been hit, only two businesses connected to my business. We bought from Petrocelli Products and Tulipano. Your business isn't connected to mine."

"I don't follow you," he said.

"If the name of the game is Business, as I've always thought," I said, "then what we're having is the side effects of a business deal. The question is who besides Rocco is dealing."

"Dealing what?" Tramontana asked.

"Not what. Who."

"But what does this guy want? I know what *I* want. I want to talk to Rocco."

So that's what it was all about. Philip Tramontana was trying to get to Uncle Rocco. Hardly anybody got to Rocco directly. Even his managers and partners had to go through Charlie Green. And Charlie wasn't keeping office hours today. So Tramontana had put out the word: he wanted to see me. Then he must have known that I had Rocco's number. How he knew it, I couldn't figure. Of

137

course he knew that Jock and I had been buddies, for we'd occasionally stopped in at the Bon Bon when we were just bumming around in the afternoon or on an off night.

"So call Rocco," I said.

"I don't know his private number."

"And you want me to call him for you."

"I'd appreciate it."

"All right. But first, do you mind if I ask a few questions, Mr. Tramontana?"

"Of course."

"It's about a movie Jock made, called *Sweet Life.*"

"Sure," Tramontana said. "The three girls out there now, the dancers, they were in that. They did a lot of loops for him too. He never paid them."

Tramontana, a/k/a Phil the Pimp, was a sick-looking thing, pale and thin, red-eyed, slack-jawed, and worried. Nose candy no longer got him high; it nowadays depressed him. And it gave him a runny nose. He lived with a handkerchief in his hand. His brains had turned to water.

"Who has copies of *Sweet Life?*"

"I don't know," he said. "Rocco, maybe, some of the movie managers . . ."

"And the other movies Jock made? Who would have them?"

He said, "You mean the loops? Most of the shops around here."

"Not the loops," I said. "I mean regular movies."

Tramontana said, "I didn't know he made any more. I just knew about *Sweet Life* and the loops. Who'd he use in the others? I wonder why he didn't come to me."

"I'll call Rocco for you," I said. "But first I'd like to make another call."

138

"Feel free," he said.

I picked up the phone and dialed Actor's Chapel. It rang three times before Father Vito answered. My watch said six straight up.

I said, "It's Joe."

"They're on the other line," Vito said. "Hold on." I could hear him telling his caller that he had me on the phone right now. He demanded to talk to Vickie. Apparently the caller refused. Vito insisted. Then he said, "Wait. I'll tell him." He told me. Vickie was unable to come to the phone. No explanation. "They're telling me to remind you that you have until midnight. If you haven't got the films by then, you won't see Vickie again—only pieces of her, scattered around town. . . . Joe, that's exactly the way they put it. What shall I tell them?"

"Are you talking to the same man we talked to before?"

"Yes."

"Then tell him I can deliver the films. Tell him also that if he harms Vickie, if there's a scratch on her, his boss will be dog meat before morning."

"Dear God! How can I say such a thing, Joe?"

"Say it, Father."

I heard him say it. Then he came back to me.

"I told him," he said. "He just laughed and hung up. I think you guessed it right, Joe. He does have an accent of some kind. It's very slight. If you didn't listen for it you wouldn't notice. And I think it may be Greek. I wouldn't bet on it."

"You can make book on it, Father."

"Well, I've got some good news for you, Joe. I heard from Sergeant Sweeney. He gave me a number. He said it's a safe phone. He'll wait for your call."

139

Vito then gave me a Brooklyn number. I wrote it in my address book.

"Call him for me," I said. "Tell him I'll get back to him."

"Will do. Anything else?"

"Just hang in there. It's going to hit the fan sometime tonight."

"Joe, be careful."

"Thanks, Father."

We hung up.

Tramontana said, "You were talking to a priest?"

"My father," I said.

"Your father? He must be eighty years old."

"Older than he looks," I said. "Tougher too. Now I'll call Rocco for you."

Usually Big Augie answered, but not this time. It was a man, of course, but I didn't recognize the voice. I wondered how Marco Lucarelli sounded over the phone. Though Rocco's son was our doorman at Pal Joey's, the occasion had never come up for me to talk to him over the phone or even the intercom, so far as I remembered.

I said, "This is Harold Williams. May I speak to Mr. Lucarelli, please?"

The man said, "One moment, sir."

In a moment, after some circuitry clattered into place, Rocco growled, "Where are you?"

I said, "The Bon Bon Bar. Your manager asked me to get in touch with you."

"What about?"

"He's worried about what's happening. He's afraid the Bon Bon might be next. I think he needs reassurance."

"Put him on. I'll talk to him."

"I will," I said. "But first I'd like to tell you a quick way to stop what's happening."

"Yeah? Go on."

"It's time to turn over those films, Rocco. That'll bring peace."

"I don't know what you're talking about. Put Phil on. Let me talk to him."

I handed the phone to Tramontana and stood up. I watched him as he listened to Rocco. He listened a long time, saying nothing.

Then he said, "I don't know, Mr. Lucarelli, sir. I don't know if I can do that."

He listened some more, glanced at me, tried again to beg off from whatever Rocco was telling him to do, then hunched his shoulders and turned his swivel chair so his back was to me. I unbuttoned my coat and jacket. He began to ease a desk drawer open with his right hand. His left still held the phone. He was still listening, or seemed to be. I slipped my hand inside my jacket, felt the butt of Big Augie's .45, and waited. When I saw Tramontana reach into the drawer, I pulled the Colt and touched the muzzle to the back of his head.

"Don't try it," I told him.

He took his right hand out of the drawer. I reached in and found a snub-nosed Colt Cobra .38 Special, much too fine a piece for a punk like this. I put it in my pocket, stuck my .45 back in my belt, and took the phone away from him.

"He tried," I told Rocco. "God knows he tried. I'll call you later and let you know when and where we make the exchange."

"What exchange?"

"All the films, and all copies, for Vickie and peace. Be ready when I call, Rocco."

I hung up.

141

Tramontana said, "I'm sorry, Mr. Streeter, but you know how it is. Rocco's my boss. He tells me to do something . . . You understand."

"Sure I do," I said. "He tells you to kiss his ass, you pucker up."

As I walked out of the joint I gave the two girls on the runway a big wink, forgetting I was wearing dark glasses. I wondered why they didn't react. I didn't see Olga in the room. I couldn't think at first of a reason why they shouldn't be friendly. I knew them, each of them, as well as any man can know a hooker. We'd always had high times together. But then I could see how maybe they now figured that since I was Jock's partner in Pal Joey's, it was reasonable to assume I was in with him in other things, like making porn flicks, and therefore shared responsibility for not having paid them. They'd worked in *Sweet Life* and not been paid, according to Tramontana. I'd never thought of Jock as cheap. But now I did think about it, and I recalled that he was always slow to pick up a tab, and tight with tips. The more I thought about it, the angrier I got. Beating a labor bill is beneath contempt, in my scale of values. Cheating those poor girls out of their hard-earned money was about as low as a man could sink.

❦ 16 ❧

I HAD TO WAIT for the Bentley when I got outside, since I'd told Andrew to circle the block until I appeared. I didn't want to stand at the curb in that flock of freaks, the sleazy pimps, psycho transvestites, male prosses, so I walked up the block to the corner of Forty-third Street and watched for the Bentley.

I was looking down the avenue when a black '75 Eldorado with yellow New Jersey plates pulled up to the curb in front of the Bon Bon. First Big Augie Benedetto got out, his left arm in cast and sling, and opened Rocco's door with his good hand. Uncle Rocco got out, and the two of them went into the bar.

Just then the Bentley came cruising slowly along and I stepped quickly into the street. Andrew stopped, and I got in, telling him to take me to the corner of Eighth Avenue and Twenty-eighth Street. He turned left on Forty-third and headed for Ninth Avenue.

As we rode I thought about Uncle Rocco's sudden appearance. He certainly couldn't have come all the way from Short Hills, New Jersey. He must have been nearby when we were talking on the phone. Had to be. Meaning he had a patch board for his car phone so that calls to his home in Jersey could be transmitted to his radiophone in the car. This would give him great mobility. He could be right around the corner.

I called the Brooklyn number. Sergeant Sweeney answered on the first ring. No mistaking that bog trotter's accent.

I said, "Do you know who this is?"

He said, "I'm not sure."

"Father gave me your number."

"Right. I know who you are."

"Can we meet privately?"

"What's it about?"

"I think I'll be able to give you Jock Alfieri's killer, or at least the man behind the hit."

"So it *was* a contract?"

"I think so."

"Well, all right, then," Sweeney said. "I'm ready whenever you say."

"It'll have to be later this evening. I'll call you when I know the time and place."

"I'll wait for your call."

Good, I thought. Now if I only knew what I was doing . . .

Andrew took a left on Twenty-eighth Street and proceeded east to Eighth Avenue, where I told him to park in front of the Eurydice and wait with the motor running.

❦ 17 ❧

IT WAS THE EVENING rush hour, lots of traffic on foot and on wheels, people hurrying home like honest citizens or stopping off at a bar for some "ignorant juice," as old Matt Griffin calls booze.

I bought a potted Easter lily in a corner florist's and wrote a little gift card: "Peace. —Rocco." So far as I knew, Uncle Rocco didn't know that Gentleman John Volos was behind the murder of Jock and the hits on Petrocelli Products and Tulipano Wines and Liquors. I didn't either. But I was beginning to figure out something I thought was logical. In any case, logic had led me here. If Iovannis Volos *didn't* have Vickie . . . Perish the thought.

The Eurydice occupied the whole ground floor of the building, facing on the avenue and the street, with big plate-glass windows on both sides. A larger-than-life-size five-color neon sign depicting a belly dancer in motion hung over the entrance on the avenue. The big windows were painted with landscapes and seascapes of the Greek islands by some artist of lesser talent than El Greco. A doorman in livery stood by the entrance. In his uniform he looked like a Greek colonel, except for the red fez with golden tassel. The size of the bulge under his left shoulder bespoke a large-caliber pacifier. He had rushed to open the door of my Bentley when I drove up, and he'd seemed a bit disconcerted when I didn't go into the club but walked on up the block to the corner. He seemed no less disconcerted now that I was returning with a potted Easter lily, but he saluted and opened the door for me.

The Eurydice bar was doing a brisk business, though the dining room was empty, except for one young couple at a corner table. The waiters were mostly just standing around. Soon the barflies would begin to get hungry, and then entertainment would begin at nine-thirty with a small group of Greek musicians and a singer, and Athena would come on at ten-thirty. Right now the only entertainment was canned Greek music. It was a nice place if you like the Coney Island style, décor à la Grecque, so to speak.

I asked the head barman for the manager, Cyril Cosmos, whom I knew since I'd often dined here.

The barman said, "He expecting you?"

"Yes. Why? Busy?"

"In the kitchen. Who do I say?"

"Just tell him Rocco sent me."

The barman hadn't recognized me in my disguise, but Rocco's name got a double take, and the barman pressed a button on the backbar and spoke into a microphone: "Someone to see Mr. Cosmos."

Presently Cyril Cosmos came out of the kitchen flanked by two big Greek chefs who held their hands under their aprons. What they held in their hands was anybody's

146

guess. I guessed guns. Cosmos had to take a second look to recognize me behind the sunglasses and under the homburg. He spoke to his two chefs and they ambled back to the kitchen. He motioned me to follow him and we went through the dining room to his office at the far end, behind the dance floor and bandstand.

It was a spacious and comfortable room, windowless but air-conditioned, thickly carpeted, well appointed, equipped with full bar, and soundproof. There was no canned music in here. Iovannis Volos owned the building, a twelve-story apartment house, with the club on the ground floor. He had excellent security. There were four elevators—two for the tenants of the apartments, one for the building maintenance staff, and a private lift that went only to the penthouse and could be entered only through the club manager's office. When we were in the office I handed Cosmos the potted lily.

He set it on the desk, took the little gift card, opened its envelope, read it: " 'Peace. —Rocco.' "

He was a short, fat man with delicate features and curly black hair tipped with gray. His eyes were large, black, and droopy from eating hashish. The fat came from over-eating sweets, a habit encouraged by hashish. He was relaxed, as if half asleep. His voice was soft and slightly effeminate, the accent very Greek.

He put the little card back into its envelope and said, "Rocco send the lily? It's for Mr. Volos?"

"I'd like you to send it up," I said," and tell him I'm here. I have to see him right away. It won't wait."

He said okay, picked up the phone and pushed an inter-com button, spoke in Greek, listened, spoke again in Greek, and hung up.

"Okay," he said. "Just a minute." He pulled a knife out

147

of his coat pocket, released the switchblade, and began probing the earth around the base of the lily. Apparently satisfied the pot did not have a bomb in it, he picked it up, handed it to me, and said, "Okay, let's go." He opened the private elevator and waited for me to enter. I went in and he followed. He touched the Up button. The cage rose slowly. It had two small closed-circuit television cameras fixed into opposite corners of the roof. "Sorry about the knife," he said. "You know how it is."

I said, "No offense."

"The lily from Rocco?" he asked again.

I said, "That's right."

"He sending flowers to Mr. Volos?"

"Right."

He looked at me and at the lily and at me again, itching to ask why Uncle Rocco would be sending a lily to Gentleman John Volos, but I wasn't about to scratch his itch for him. The elevator hummed to a stop at the penthouse, the door slid open, and I walked into the foyer holding the lily pot. Cosmos was behind me.

Only one door led off the foyer. It had a judas window. I heard a tiny click and saw an eye at the peephole. Then the door opened and George Patourakis, our manager of the gambling rooms at Pal Joey's, walked into the foyer smiling and holding out his hands. I put the lily pot in them.

"Good to see you, Joe," he said.

His was the voice I'd been trying to identify, the harsh voice of the man on the telephone who had threatened to "take the broad apart" if I didn't get the movie films together by midnight. Unlike Cyril Cosmos, his accent was very slight, hardly noticeable. It was the quality of his voice, the harshness, the gruffness, that identified him. His cheeks were raked with claw marks, red and raw.

I unbuttoned my topcoat without realizing that my gesture could be misinterpreted. I wasn't going to pull Big Augie's .45 yet. I wasn't even thinking of it. There was no need at the moment.

But Cosmos said behind me, "Hold it, Mr. Streeter!"

I felt something hard prod me below the right kidney. Knife or gun, it didn't matter. I held my hands away from my body. Cosmos patted my topcoat pockets, found Tramontana's .38 Colt Cobra, took it, reached around me and patted my chest on each side, felt Jock's busted Miroku in its shoulder holster and took it too. That seemed to satisfy him. Fortunately he didn't check to see if I had a third piece stuck in my belt at the left hip. After all, who carries three guns?

George said, "Will you hold this please, Joe?" He held out the lily pot and I took it from him. He said something in Greek to Cosmos, and Cosmos gave him the Cobra and the Miroku. He spoke again in Greek and Cosmos went back into the elevator. To me George said, "You can hang your things on the hat tree." I said I'd keep them on. "Suit yourself," he said. He slipped the Cobra into his coat pocket, holding the Miroku on me. I decided to wait until we were inside with Volos. If I made my move now that door might not open. George pressed the buzzer and the door opened. He said, "Go on in."

I went in. He followed close with the gun. We entered a reception room: Oriental throw rugs on a blue-and-yellow mosaic tile floor, fine carpets hanging on the walls, casts of ancient Greek sculptures atop small Doric columns, two arched doorways with amber bead curtains, peppermint-stick wallpaper, and what I thought at first was the smell of incense, then recognized as the aroma of Greek hashish.

George said we'd wait here. I stood holding the lily pot. He held Jock's gun. We smiled at each other and waited. George Patourakis was a big man—not fat, for he apparently didn't eat hashish and sweets, and I know he didn't drink, being a professional gambler—a muscular build, about heavyweight size, thick-shouldered, strong-jawed, clean-shaven, and alert. No need to wonder why Jock and Uncle Rocco had hired him, or taken him as a manager-partner of our gambling rooms, for he knew his business. That he was Greek made no difference. Italians worked for Volos too. And anyone, Greek or Italian, could sell out as George had obviously done. It's just business. But I shouldn't say *anyone* could sell out: it takes the business turn of mind to do that.

Iovannis "Gentleman John" Volos, the Patriarch of Chelsea, came through one of the amber-curtained arches then, tall and fat, waddling like an enormous gander, smiling, dripping jewels from all fingers and both wrists.

"For me?" he said, taking the lily pot. He set it on a low coffee table and took the little envelope and opened it. He read the note aloud: " 'Peace.—Rocco.' " He smiled broadly and said to George, "Why the gun, Kukla?" It is a Greek term of endearment, meaning "doll," and *kuklaki* means little doll. George answered him in Greek, and Volos said, "Speak English! Don't be rude, Kuklaki."

"Sorry, Mr. Volos," said George. He looked at me and looked away. I don't know much Greek, but I once played a club in Piraeus called the Byron (for the poet is still honored in Greece) and of course I picked up a smattering. When I learned the word *kukla* it was understood that most male Greeks don't call each other "doll." And so George Patourakis was embarrassed. His gun hand twitched. I watched the trigger finger and thought I saw it tighten. But the gun was not pointing toward me, rather toward my feet. George was not in a hurry to shoot me. Not that I was worried. He said, "Streeter had two guns on him, Mr. Volos."

Big fat Volos looked at me sadly, and it was quite a performance, almost as good as the Greek tragedy he performed at the bar of Pal Joey's when he told me how sorry he was to learn of Jock's death.

"Joe," he said in sorrow, "is this true?"

"Not entirely," I said. "It wasn't two guns, John, it was three." He even had *me* talking stagy. I reached inside my jacket and took out Big Augie's hefty Colt .45 automatic. Even the gesture was stagy. Poor George panicked when he saw me go for the gun. He leveled the Miroku at my head and pulled the trigger. The hammer struck but no shot fired. That broken firing pin. He pulled the trigger again. Cursing frantically in Greek, he threw the gun to the floor and started to reach in his coat pocket for the Cobra. I said, "Don't do it, George."

He didn't. I told him to raise his hands a little from his sides and stand still. I took the Cobra out of his pocket and put it in mine. Then I found that he wore an Astra .25 in a belt clip on his right hip, and I took that and clipped it to my belt. I turned him around and frisked him, ankles, calves, crotch, hips, belly and back, and armpits. No more guns. He had a seven-inch switch knife in his right coat pocket. I took that too. What with four guns (three functional) and George's seven-inch scimitar, I was a walking arsenal. I wanted to kill him, but I realized that first I might want to hear what he had to say.

I told Volos to turn around and I frisked him. He was clean. I told him and George to stand close together. They did. I picked up the Miroku and put it in its holster.

"Now," I said, "take me to Vickie. Try anything stupid and I'll kill you both."

Volos led the way, George following close behind him, through a bead curtain and past a long dining room to an enormous kitchen, a replica of a good Greek country kitchen with a walk-in fireplace big enough for roasting a whole sheep. I followed as Volos waddled through the kitchen. If he tried something stupid, like grabbing a meat cleaver or a butcher knife, I'd have to shoot George first, for he walked between us, and this just might give Volos enough time to strike a blow if he was very fast. He must have thought of it, but he must also have realized that if he didn't score on the first try he'd be a dead Greek. We went on through a large pantry and into a sitting room such as a wealthy Athenian or Alexandrian would give himself: ample couches with fat gaudy pillows, a small fountain sprinkling in a corner, some drums and a bazouki in another corner, a low brass coffee table with a tall, slender four-hose nargileh, some pieces of black hashish waiting on the brass ring around the brazier, bottles of retsina, ouzo, mavrodaphne, and four ram's-horn cups mounted on silver stands.

Vickie was sitting on an ottoman by the fountain as we came in, and when she saw me she leaped up and ran to me crying, throwing herself on me, crying and laughing, "Joe! Oh, Joe!" Over and over, laughing and crying. I kept my gun hand free. She wasn't hurt except for a mouse and a slightly swollen lower lip, a few shoulder bruises, a set of finger bruises on her throat, and some rope burns on her wrists. Nothing really heavy. Her clothes looked as if

152

she'd slept in them. She was wearing her favorite costume, full skirt and wide-necked blouse. Superb neck and shoulders, very ballerina. Bruised now with blue blotches.

I asked her if George had made those marks, and she said yes.

I told George and Volos to sit on one of the couches, close together. They did.

Volos said, "What are you going to do, Joe? I thought you came in peace. The lily—didn't Rocco . . . ?"

I said, "Shut up. Who else is in the apartment?"

"Only Athena," said Volos.

"And Charlie Green," said Vickie. "He's dead. They killed him."

Volos said, "Not *they*, dear girl. George did it. You saw him. *I* never touched the man."

"It was an accident," George said.

Vickie said, "He was holding Charlie's head under water in the bathroom, in the toilet bowl. He held him under too long."

I asked Volos, "Where's the body?"

"In the kitchen," he said. "In the big freezer."

I asked Vickie, "And where's Athena?"

"In her bedroom, I think," she said.

"Can you bring her in here?" I got out the Astra that I'd taken from George, stuck my .45 in my belt, checked the Astra, made sure there was one in the chamber and the gun was cocked, and gave it to Vickie. She said she wouldn't need it. Athena was friendly, not like her father or George. I said, "Take it anyway."

She did. She went through another bead-curtained archway and I turned to Volos.

"You're Athena's *father?*" I said.

"Her natural father," he said. "I knew her mother many

153

years ago in Alexandria. She was a dancer in one of my places. When she had the child I retired her and gave her a partnership in the club. She raised Athena and taught her the dance. I kept in touch and when Athena's mother died a year ago I brought the girl here. Everyone thinks she's my mistress. We both find it convenient. It enhances my image, and it keeps the men at a proper distance. Few would be brave enough to make a play for the Patriarch's woman."

"Few men," I said. "But a few, nevertheless."

"Assuredly," Volos said and sighed. "Athena is not a child. I ask only that she be discreet."

"And she was indiscreet," I said. "She let Jock Alfieri photograph her in the nude. They made a movie, *Danse du Ventre*. And that's what it's all about."

"Precisely," said Volos. "I want that film. Have you got it?"

"Rocco has the films, *Danse du Ventre* and the others," I said, hoping I was right. "I'm here to set up the exchange. You have Charlie Green's account books?"

"Yes."

"Good," I said. "I have all *I* want personally. I have Vickie. But I'm also involved in those account books as co-owner of Pal Joey's. So let me see them. I need to know you've really got them before I set up the exchange with Rocco."

"Dear boy," said Volos. He smiled at me as if I were a foolish child. "If I show them to you, you'll take them and I'll never get that film. You have the guns, you have the power, but if you kill me . . ."

"Kill you," I said. "Or make you wish I'd kill you."

"Torture?" said Volos. "You couldn't, Joe."

154

Couldn't, eh? Maybe not. In any case, I had what I wanted, my Vickie. If trouble came from those account books I could always lam out of the country. I still had the little chamois bag of Brazilian rocks; no longer a fortune, but enough.

Vickie came back with Athena then, Vickie holding the Astra loosely, Athena looking drawn, tense. She glared at Volos with murder in her eyes. I told her to sit on the other side of the room from Volos and George. She did and Vickie sat beside her.

"Athena," I said, "were you having an affair with Jock Alfieri?"

She broke up, doubled over, sobbing. Then she suddenly straightened and spat Greek curses at Volos, who looked as if she'd struck him in the face. She reached for Vickie's gun, and Vickie moved it away from her. Volos said something to her in Greek. I told him to speak English.

"Alfieri was trying to blackmail me," Volos said. "He threatened to put Athena's film in the movie theaters. Fifty thousand dollars!"

"You could have paid it," I said.

"Only a fool pays a blackmailer," Volos said. "He would have come back later with a copy of the film for sale, and then another copy, and another. . . ."

"So you had him killed."

"But of course," he said, and he smiled a fat smile as if to say: What else?

"Who got the contract?"

"Now really, Joe, you don't expect me to . . ."

"I could shoot you now, John. Why not?"

"It was Lieutenant Maginnis. He handled it. I don't

know what arrangements he made. I paid him five thousand in front. I owe him another five. He engaged the hitter."

"There's more to it," I said. "Someone had to get into our office at the club, open the safe. . . . Suppose you begin at the beginning. And try telling the truth. It could save your life. You know, Kuklaki, I ought to shoot you for what you've done to Vickie, not to mention killing my dog."

Vickie said, "Schatzi!"

"Dead," I said. "Shot between the eyes. Same hitter who killed Jock."

"I'm sorry," Volos said. "I didn't know. But Vickie isn't seriously hurt. Besides, I didn't handle her. George did."

I snapped off a shot, putting it in the wall behind them and right between their heads. The roar of the Colt .45 is enough to scare the dead. George looked faint, and Volos shook all over like a mountain of strawberry mousse.

"All right!" he cried. "All right! That's enough! Just let me catch my breath and I'll tell you, all of it, but I can't breathe."

True, he seemed very short of breath. Fear can do that to a man, especially if he's old and fat and his heart's working too hard anyway. I waited. George seemed to be asleep. In fact, he'd fainted. His clawed cheeks were livid.

When Volos was breathing more evenly I told him, "Now, John."

"I got a call from Jock Alfieri," he said, "a few weeks ago. He said he'd made a movie of Athena dancing in the nude and asked if I'd like to buy it. He came at me just like that, straight to the point. I told him I'd buy it of course, and I stalled him. I needed time to talk to Athena and if necessary to make arrangements for handling him. The problem was to get hold of the film and all copies of

156

it before killing him, or possibly at the same time. Killing him would have been the easy part. Getting the film and its copies, however . . . So I consulted George. He knew the layout of Pal Joey's and how you people ran the place. We needed keys in order to get into Jock's photography studio. Athena had told me that's where we'd probably find her film. She gave me a detailed description of the studio, the nude photographs hanging on the walls, the file of negatives, the cross-index card file, the cans of movies he'd made. . . ."

Athena suddenly stood up and pulled the upper part of her dress down around her waist. It was a knit sheath, sleeveless, and it came down easily. Under it she was naked. What we saw besides her bare breasts, which were fine, was a crosshatch of red welts. Whip marks. Her sapphire eyes blazed blue fire.

"*That's* why I told him!" she cried. "My own father did this to me!"

"When?" I asked.

"When he wanted to know about Jock's studio," she said. "He told me Jock was trying to blackmail him with my movie. *I* don't care about this goddamn movie. He could show it to the whole world, what do I care?"

"But *I* care," Volos said. "I don't want every man in New York City looking at my daughter naked."

I said, "What I meant, Athena, was when did John whip you? When did he make those marks? It had to be recently."

"It was day before yesterday," she said.

"But you were at my club with him last night," I said. "You forgive easily."

"Oh, it's not the first time he's whipped me," she said. She looked at me steadily for a long beat, then said, "I

157

didn't know he was going to kill Jock."

I said to John, "You whipped the information out of your daughter, she told you the details about Jock's studio, and George told you about our setup with keys. So how did you plan to get the keys?"

"From Green, since he's your lawyer-accountant," said Volos. "But first I thought about the copies of the film. Athena said Jock had made several films, some of them commercial. . . ."

I asked Athena, "Did Jock show you his other films?"

"Yes," she said.

"And you told your father about them?"

"He made me tell him everything."

Volos said, "I assumed that Jock's uncle was in this with him. I knew he was in the business, of course, topless bars, peep shows, and porn movie theaters. . . ."

"You knew more than I did," I said.

"Is that so?" He smiled skeptically. "I had assumed you were in it with them. Athena said Jock told her you knew nothing about it, but I was sure you did, so I decided to use you as a go-between in my negotiations with Rocco."

"You kidnapped Vickie as a weapon to use on me. But why snatch Charlie Green?"

"I thought he might have a set of keys or know how I could get one. I was right. He knew of a spare set kept in your office safe. He gave me the combination to the safe. George got the combination out of him. And he had a key to the office. That was all I needed. I gave the office key and the safe combination to Maginnis, plus five thousand dollars on account, the other five thousand to be paid on delivery of the films, the negative file, and all the female nude photos."

"You wanted all of them," I said, "as a cover for the ones

158

you really needed. Did Maginnis know which ones you really were after? Did he know that Athena had made a movie and posed for nude stills?"

"No, not then. He probably knows now."

"Why did you pick Maginnis for the contract?"

"I knew through George that Maginnis was on your pad, taking protection for the card rooms. He was in a position to set Jock up. Anyway, you see, the job didn't go off right. The hitter got Alfieri, but he missed the films. So I figure Uncle Rocco has the films."

"So you've been putting on the heat. You don't play around, do you?"

"You tell Rocco for me, Joe, and make him believe it, if he doesn't come across with Athena's film and all copies, I'll burn him down, I'll plow him under, and I'll sow the land with salt." His smile was chilly. "Believe me, Joe," he said. "And make Rocco believe me."

Suddenly the unmistakable racket of machine guns rattled like strings of giant firecrackers in the street thirteen floors below. Volos turned toward a curtained arch, heaved himself to his feet, and headed for the archway. I told Vickie to wait here and keep her gun on George, and I went after Volos, following him through an adjoining room and an outer door onto the roof.

We leaned on the parapet and looked down into Eighth Avenue just in time to see three Checker cabs streak away from in front of the Eurydice, machine guns still blazing from the cabs' windows. One turned into Twenty-eighth Street and went east, one went up to Twenty-ninth and took a left and headed west, and the other sped on up the avenue.

A familiar-looking black Eldorado across the avenue was slowly pulling away from the curb, joining the uptown traffic. I glanced at Volos. He apparently hadn't noticed the black car. He was looking straight down the façade of the building. There was a lot of shattered glass on the sidewalk. A pedestrian was down. Several people and a cop were bending over him. Another cop was in the corner phone booth. Sirens were beginning to howl nearby. The first blue-and-white came whooping out of Twenty-eighth Street from the west and skidded to a stop in front of the club. It stopped behind the Bentley.

The Bentley seemed to be all right. Andrew was standing by it, watching the action. More sirens were howling in the distance.

A phone rang in the room we'd just left. Volos hurried to answer it. I followed him close. After he'd said hello he spoke Greek, listened, asked questions in Greek, and then lined it out for me. The whole front of the Eurydice had been shot out, a waiter and two patrons killed, several others injured. The club was a shambles. The doorman didn't get a good description of the gunmen in the three Checker cabs, but he thought they looked Italian.

I wondered exactly when Rocco had found out that Volos was behind Jock's murder and the Petrocelli and Tulipano raids. Had he known all along? I didn't think so. If he'd known, he'd have hit back at Volos long since. So when did he find out? And how?

"Rocco," said Volos. "Peace, eh? I'll crucify him." He laughed harshly. "I'll plant that lily on his grave."

We heard a shot from the sitting room. I prodded Volos with the .45, shoving him ahead of me. We found George dead on the floor, lying on his belly, head turned to one side. Just above the left cheek, where the claw marks began, at the hairline, a small dark hole oozed blood.

There was no powder burn around the hole.

"He tried to rush me," Vickie said.

But the position of the bullet hole indicated that he'd not been facing her when he was shot. He'd been shot from the left side. I looked at Vickie. She looked straight at me, brown eyes big with innocence. I tried Athena, but she just looked away.

"Those claw marks," I said. "Did you make those, Vickie?"

"*I* did," said Athena. "When he hit Vickie, I struck him with my fingernails."

I could see how it must have been. Volos seemed to have had a problem with his natural daughter. She didn't like his methods, especially since he'd put out the contract on her lover, Jock Alfieri, a cad but still her lover. He was behind the beating of a woman, Vickie, and the torture of a man until he was killed, poor Charlie Green. Hers was an *un*natural father, and if ever she'd loved him, she hated him now. Because of a nude movie she had made he was prepared to commit acts of torture and murder.

"Vickie and I are leaving now," I said to Volos. "I'll get back to you after I talk to Rocco. There'll be an exchange sometime this evening. His account books for your daughter's movie. I'll give you the details later. Meanwhile what about cops? They'll be swarming up here anytime now. Can you handle them? Will you be available tonight?"

"I won't be here when they come," he said. "I have other apartments in the building."

"How can we get out of here?" I asked.

"Only one way, the side door. You'll see it when you get down to the office.

Athena said, "Joe, take me with you. Please?"

Volos got to his feet quicker than you'd have thought he could.

"No!" he said. His fat jaw dropped open and his eyes bugged out. "Athena!"

He spoke to her rapidly in Greek. She moved toward a bead-curtained arch, and he moved to cut her off.

I cranked off another shot, putting this one in the big brass nargileh on the coffee table and knocking it across the room. The racket was deafening. It stopped Gentleman John.

As I left with the two girls, he was pouring himself a horn of ouzo. Poor Patriarch, he had a problem. Two problems: George Patourakis and Charlie Green. Maybe he'd use that big walk-in fireplace in the kitchen, big enough to roast a whole sheep. It would take a while, but eventually both George and Charlie could be reduced to smoke and ashes.

Gentleman John had a yet bigger problem: not so much Uncle Rocco as one Joe Streeter.

❦ 18 ❧

I HALF EXPECTED to see cops in the office when we came out of the private elevator. There were some in the bar and the dining room. Cyril Cosmos was on the phone. He waved us to the side door. It didn't lead into the club, but out to the street.

Andrew would be waiting with the Bentley, engine running, in front of the club entrance on the avenue, around the corner. By now the cops would be interrogating him. I told Vickie and Athena we'd avoid Eighth Avenue and walk over to Seventh and catch a cab. They didn't know about Andrew, and there wasn't time to explain.

How did Rocco find out that Volos was behind the murder of Jock and the hits on Petrocelli Products and Tulipano Wines and Liquors? Unintentionally I set it up myself. When I met with Rocco on the roof of the Port Authority Bus Terminal he hadn't known Volos was behind the whole caper. Neither had I. And I hadn't found out for certain until I actually went to see Volos. I figured that if Rocco had somehow been tailing me he'd have deduced the answers as he followed my progress from Sullivan's Gym to the Sherry-Netherland to Valentino's apartment, each time eliminating suspect persons who'd been involved in Jock's porn movies. If Rocco had the films he'd know who was in each one, and he'd know that when I left Valentino's place I had only one place left to go. He would doubtless have got to the Eurydice before me had he not been delayed by my surprise visit to the Bon Bon Bar. So who could have been providing him with information? Who but Andrew? Using the car phone.

And how had Rocco got onto Andrew? Easy. Now see how neatly I set myself up. I'd told Rocco he could get in touch with me through Father Vito. So of course Rocco staked out Actor's Chapel, probably faster than it took me to get from the Port Authority building to the chapel. And when I later rode off in a chauffeured Bentley, all Rocco or his man had to do was follow and wait until I'd left the car for one of the afternoon's visits, and then make his pitch. Andrew probably went for a hundred-dollar bill. Adiós, Andrew.

My immediate problem was where to stash Vickie and Athena while I took care of the night's business. Volos was no problem now. He'd be busy for a while organizing his forces for the coming exchange: film for account books. Uncle Rocco was the problem. I'd seen a familiar black Eldorado pulling away from the curb across the avenue from the Eurydice just as the three armed Checker cabs roared away. If I took Vickie and Athena to Actor's Chapel, a stakeout might be waiting. Rocco had tried to kill me on the Port Authority roof. He might try again. Or he might snatch Vickie and Athena and use them as weapons against both me and Volos. Crazy, both of them, the Guinea and the Greek.

So I called Matt Griffin from a luncheonette around the corner on Seventh Avenue, and he agreed to put the girls in a safe suite. I hailed a Checker and we got in. I told the driver to take us to the Hotel Commodore, the entrance on the Park Avenue ramp, and I spent the next few minutes getting to know Vickie again. Her bruised lip was tender to the kiss. Marvelous. Her black eye gave her a roguish look, very stimulating. I was kissing away her neck and shoulder bruises when I heard Athena sobbing.

Vickie said to her, "You poor dear, I'm so sorry. Joe and I just didn't think."

She put an arm around the Egyptian girl and comforted her. I was thinking no cheap crook like my ex-partner Jock Alfieri deserved the tears of such a fine lass.

Matt was at the entrance when I handed the girls over. I held the cab. Matt said there were still a couple of detectives hanging about the lobby. I told him to phone the girls' room number to Father Vito when he'd got them installed. Old Matt's reunion with Vickie was like a grandfather's with his granddaughter. True love. Actually the Egyptian was the real beauty. She had a face and figure that could start wars. Vickie was a ballerina, after all, very slender. That's nice too, but I thought that when this was all over and Vickie had gone back to Chicago, maybe I'd see about Athena. She was a lot of belly dancer.

I left the girls with Matt and told the cabby to take me to Twenty-third Street and Eighth Avenue, and when we got there I had him go up the avenue. As we passed the Eurydice, traffic slowed because of all the rubbernecks ogling the scene, three ambulances from two hospitals,

Roosevelt and Saint Vincent's, a dozen blue-and-whites, several unmarked cars, gold shields everywhere flashing in the red glow of sunset. An ambulance was pulling away from the curb in front of the club, heading up the avenue to Roosevelt with a squad car clearing the way, siren whooping. Pedestrians were crowding around, cops were trying to shoo them away. The Eurydice was a total wreck. Even the neon sign with the belly dancer had been shot away.

I had the driver continue on up to Fiftieth Street, then take a right. As we passed Pal Joey's it was clear, no more cops in front. No way to see if there were any inside. I paid off the cabby on the east side of Broadway and made my phone calls from the bank of booths on the southeast corner.

First I called Father Vito and told him I was through with Elite Limousine Service for the day. If he would pay Andrew off I'd reimburse him. Andrew should be coming along anytime now.

"And Vickie?" asked Vito.

"She's all right," I said. "I've put her in a safe place." I could hear him sigh with relief. "It was Volos," I told him. "There's more to it, but I'll have to tell you when I see you."

Then I called Rocco and told him Volos was ready to deal: the account books for the films, *all* of them. He didn't argue. I didn't explain. Those account books could put him in prison. The films could not.

"Did he have Jock killed?" he asked.

I said, "Yes. He also hit the Petrocelli and Tulipano places. He really wants those films, Rocco."

"Okay," Rocco said. "He can have them. All I want is peace. How we gonna do it?"

166

I said, "How soon can you have the films ready?"

"I got them ready now," he said.

"All right," I told him. "Bring them to the place we met before, right? One hour?"

"Be there," he said. "And bring Charlie."

I called Volos and asked if it was cool to talk. He said not to worry. I figured he was in one of his other apartments in the Eurydice building, with a special phone hookup. So I told him where and when.

And I added, "Uncle Rocco wants you to bring Charlie Green."

I heard the fat man laughing.

"He doesn't know Green's—ah, you know . . . ?"

"No," I said. "He doesn't know."

"I like your sense of humor, Kuklaki."

I thought he'd really appreciate my sense of humor in about an hour. I phoned Sergeant Sweeney and asked him how soon he could meet me in Times Square.

"Forty minutes," he said. "Where exactly?"

"By the statue of Father Duffy. Alone, Sergeant."

He agreed. I checked the time, then went down to the Howard Johnson restaurant on the west side of the square and took a seat where I could watch the Duffy statue. I had a coffee and Danish. I dawdled over this stuff, then lit a cigar and waited some more. Beautiful old Broadway. I saw Irv Cohen, the shylock who used to work out of Jack Dempsey's before they shut it down. He was actually feeding pigeons by the statue. It just goes to show you, nobody's all bad, not even a shy.

The sergeant was on time and alone. He might have phoned ahead and arranged a trap, but I didn't think so. Anyway, I really had nothing to worry about. Commander Fitzroy's murder warrant wouldn't stick. I had a witness now. Vickie could testify that she'd heard Volos confess the whole thing, how he'd put out the contract on Jock, how he'd kidnapped Vickie and Charlie Green, the whole megillah.

Well, not quite the whole thing. I still didn't know who'd actually hit Jock and killed Schatzi. So Maginnis had the contract, but I knew he hadn't pulled the trigger. The hitter was someone wearing a black rat's-tail mustache, goatee, and sideburns, a small person in a sharp suit, wide-brimmed hat, and pink sunglasses. Someone agile. The killer had gone up the fire escape very nimbly.

I thought Maginnis must have hired more than one person. One to kill Jock. And one or more to do the inside job—first the office safe, then Jock's studio, then my apartment when the films weren't found in the studio.

The hit couldn't have been planned with my gun in mind. Not likely. That had to come as an afterthought, say when they were going through the place looking for those cans of movie film and not finding them. That would be when they found my gun and decided what a good joke it would be on old Joe Streeter to use his P-38. So one or two persons carried the negative file and the nude still photos away, perhaps over the roofs or perhaps down the inside stairway to the street, while the hitter went down the fire escape and shot Jock with my gun. And with Lieutenant Maginnis's timely cooperation, of course.

Mike Maginnis should be the one who knew who the actual hitter was.

I looked for a gopher. There were several types on the street, any one of whom would run the errand for a dollar. I picked my man, an old wino, dirty and unshaven. He'd been going through a trash container. I left the restaurant, collared my man, gave him a five-dollar bill and pointed out Sergeant Sweeney.

"Tell that man Joe said to meet him in Shubert Alley right away," I said.

The wino said, "Shubert Alley. Gotcha. Joe says meet him in Shubert Alley right away. Okay? Got it."

He clutched the five in his grimy fist and headed across Broadway to Duffy Square. He approached Sweeney and made his spiel. The sergeant looked around trying to locate me. Then he left Duffy Square and crossed Broadway, heading for Shubert Alley, with me thirty paces behind him. I caught him up before we got to the Alley.

"I'm in a hurry," I told him. "We'll walk while we talk."

"Where we going?" Sweeney said.

"To the Port Authority Bus Terminal. Do you know Gentleman John Volos?"

"Yes."

"He put out the contract on Jock Alfieri."

"Why?"

"Business."

"Who made the hit?"

"That's what I'm working on."

"You don't know?"

"I'll know later tonight."

"How do you know Volos put out the contract?"

"He told me. I have two witnesses."

"He told you that much, but he didn't tell you who got the contract?"

"Lieutenant Michael Maginnis."

"I don't believe it."

"Believe it, Sergeant. He's a crooked cop. He was on our pad. Protection for the card rooms upstairs."

"You have card rooms in Pal Joey's?"

"*Had,* Sergeant. They won't be reopening."

"But if Maginnis was on your pad, as you say, why would he take a contract on Alfieri? That's not business."

"Sure it is. Volos bought him."

By now we were walking down Eighth Avenue toward the terminal.

"But Maginnis doesn't fit the physical description you gave me of the hitter—small, slender. . . ."

"He only handled the contract. He didn't make the hit himself."

"I don't think I want any part of this, Streeter. They pulled me off the case. I could get my ass in a sling."

"Come *on,* Sergeant! You know you'd love to collar Maginnis. I can give him to you tied up like an Easter basket. All you'll have to do is be there."

"Where?"

"My apartment, if there's no fuzz still hanging around."

"They finished up this afternoon."

"Good. Eleven o'clock?"

"Streeter, if anybody should ask, this conversation never happened. I'll be at your place at eleven. But when I show, I'm prepared to say I've come to arrest you for the murder of Jock Alfieri. And I'll do it, Streeter. You better not goof."

"Don't worry. You can start the action yourself, Sergeant, by making sure Maginnis is there. Tell him an informant told you I have an ironclad alibi and I can be found in my own apartment after eleven tonight. That will make him come to me. He won't come with a squad, he'll be alone. To kill me. And when I confront him with my two witnesses, he'll have nothing to lose by killing us

170

all. So you'd better bring a squad. He's a cop, after all, armed and dangerous."

"What's in it for you, Streeter?"

"I get off the hook for Jock's murder. I put Maginnis away for life on charges of conspiracy to commit murder. And I get my nightclub back again."

"I think I see what you're driving at," Sweeney said. "I know about the Lucarelli connection. How do you figure to deal with Uncle Rocco? He was his nephew's backer, right? That makes him your partner now, doesn't it?"

"Not for long, Sergeant. Stick around."

"What do you mean?"

We had reached the front of the terminal by now.

"Just stick around. Wait right here for twenty minutes. You're about to become the right man in the right place at the right time. You'll be able to bag both Volos and Rocco for all kinds of homicide. It's Volos who's been hitting Rocco's businesses. Do you know about this afternoon's raid on the Eurydice?"

"I heard."

"That was Uncle Rocco striking back at Volos."

"Gang war?"

"With another confrontation coming up in a few minutes: Rocco and Volos, in person."

"Right here? On the street?"

"On the parking roof. You'd better call in, get some assistance. Do it now, Sergeant."

"What are *you* going to do, Streeter?"

"I'm going to watch the fun."

He went to a call box, and I went in to the elevators. When I came out of the elevator on the roof there was no one in the foyer. I took a long, careful look through the

171

glass doors onto the parking area. A few commuters were going home, some early celebrants were coming in. All innocent bystanders. I hoped they understood the rules. When innocent bystanders hear gunfire they are supposed to assume the prone position and make a low profile.

I waited by the elevators. Presently I saw Uncle Rocco's black Eldorado come off the ramp, followed by two other Cadillacs, and proceed slowly around the roof. When Rocco's car stopped by me I told him to continue until he was three-quarters of the way around. Then wait. His son Marco and Big Augie Benedetto rode with him. I didn't know the men in the other cars.

I walked back toward the ramp. Volos was arriving in an Imperial with two Thunderbirds behind him. I stopped him a quarter of the way around the roof, thus placing the width of the entire parking area between the two parties.

Volos had Cyril Cosmos with him. I told Volos to have Cyril bring the ledgers to the elevator foyer as soon as he saw Rocco's man start with the film cans. Then I went back to Rocco and told him how we'd do it. He had Marco carry the film cans. I helped him. I saw Cosmos start out with the two ledgers. We all met at the foyer.

I examined the ledgers. They looked real. I opened the film can labeled *Danse du Ventre*, checked the first few frames, holding the film up against the brightly lighted foyer. My hands were shaky, just a little.

I told Marco and Cosmos to give Rocco and Volos a message: *I* would hold the ledgers and film cans. Marco and Cosmos protested that I had no right. I showed them my right, the big Colt automatic. They trotted off to report to their bosses.

I dropped the Colt in a coat pocket, then took off my

pants belt and strung the handles of the film cans on it. I could see a lot of agitated talking at Volos's and Rocco's cars.

Marco came running back to me, yelling as he ran, "Where's Charlie? Rocco wants Charlie!"

I said, "See that Imperial? You run over there and tell Volos that Rocco wants Charlie. Tell him he can't get off the roof until he delivers."

"But *you're* supposed to handle this, Joe!"

"Forget it, kid. Go tell Volos like I said. He'll turn Charlie loose. Don't worry. Unless he's buried him someplace . . ."

Marco looked at me as if I'd gone mad. He backed away, then turned and ran for Rocco's car, not Volos's. I saw Rocco looking toward me as Marco spoke to him. I was beginning to sweat.

I put the two ledgers under my left arm, slung the belted film cans over my right shoulder, and backed around the edge of the foyer. I wondered who'd start the shooting.

One of Volos's cars pulled ahead of his Imperial and moved slowly around the roof. I waited and watched. The men in Rocco's cars also watched. When it was close to Rocco's car, a rear door opened and Charlie Green came tumbling out, doubled up like a fetus and frozen solid.

The driver dug out of there as if his Thunderbird was a dragster, with a squeal of burning rubber, and one of Rocco's cars was right behind him, crowding his rear bumper.

Guns poked out of Rocco's other cars and began shooting at Volos's cavalcade, and Volos's men returned the shots. Car doors burst open and men began piling out to get better fields of fire. It was the bicentennial year's no doubt greatest pyrotechnic display and one of the loudest. Machine guns, carbines, heavy-caliber handguns roared. Shotguns boomed.

I watched from the protection of the edge of the foyer, ducking back when wild (or maybe not so wild) shots crashed through the heavy glass doors, scattering shards of glass like snow in a blizzard. I saw Cyril Cosmos go down, then Marco Lucarelli. I saw Big Augie trying to shoot right-handed, and someone got him. He fell backward between parked cars. I saw machine gun fire stitching the back of the Imperial and assumed Volos was hit. I saw the same thing happen to Rocco's car. Then someone lobbed a grenade and the Imperial exploded in flames. Exit Gentleman John Volos, ex-Patriarch of Chelsea.

The two cars that had been racing toward the exit ramp had collided, blocking the exit and trapping everyone on the roof. Just beautiful. I was shaking and sweating. And laughing deep inside.

When I came out of the down elevator on the main level, Sergeant Sweeney and a lot of uniformed cops were going into the up elevator. Sweeney saw me just as his elevator's doors were closing. I gave him a friendly, encouraging smile and handed my load to a porter. My nerves were jangling like a busted piano. The guns had long since stopped on the roof, but not in my head. I heard them in my skull bones.

❧ 19 ❧

As my cab pulled away from the terminal building the blue-and-whites were screaming all over Times Square, Hell's Kitchen, and Chelsea. The gun battle on the roof of the terminal must have been heard from the Hudson to the East River, from Penn Station to Columbus Circle. It was a lovely war. I had seen at least six men hit, most probably including Volos and Rocco, though I couldn't be sure. If those two dolls hadn't shot the sawdust out of each other, Sweeney would be escorting them to Roosevelt Hospital or to Saint Vincent's and from there to the prison ward at Bellevue. Or the city morgue. In any case, they were out of my hair. I could go back to running an honest nightclub, the way it had been before Jock Alfieri and his uncle Rocco bought in. Or maybe I'd quit business altogether. Go back on the road, playing around the world, as I'd always done before I got ambitious.

You couldn't tell by looking at Pal Joey's that there'd been a murder last night. Two murders, if you considered the killing of Schatzi as murder. I did.

I paid off the cabby, unlocked the street door to the upper floors, and shlepped the ledgers and film cans up to my place. Schatzi would have been barking by now, hearing my footsteps on the fourth-floor landing. I let myself into the empty apartment.

I took the Colt out of my topcoat pocket, put it in my jacket, and hung up the hat and coat. Then I phoned Father Vito and asked him to go to the Hotel Commodore and bring Vickie and Athena to my apartment before eleven. He needed to know what was happening, so I told him a little about the shoot-out on the Port Authority roof. My next objective, I told him, was the actual killer of Jock and Schatzi, and I expected to handle that problem this evening. He said he'd be glad to help in any way he could.

Then I called Mady and Hub, Chico and Honey, and the Garay twins, and told them they could come and get their films tomorrow afternoon. I also called the girls at the Bon Bon and invited them to come to my apartment tonight at eleven o'clock for their films. I didn't speak to Marie, Judy, and Olga personally. I gave the message to their club manager, and pimp, Phil Tramontana.

When I'd finished these calls, I still had over an hour to myself. I poured a double Rémy and took it to the piano. I vamped awhile. Schatzi had enjoyed the piano. She'd get up on the piano bench with me and sit listening and smiling, from time to time uttering a small, singy sound. She particularly liked slow blues. When I'd finished my drink I was hungry, so I went to the kitchen and got out some fried chicken that I'd stashed in the fridge a couple of days before. Schatzi would have got the neck. She loved crunching the neck bones. I cracked a can of ale and carried the platter of chicken and the ale into the parlor and set them on the bar.

The cans of film lay in a jumble in the middle of the floor. I untied the belt that strung the handles together, then threaded the belt through my pants loops and cinched it up. I took the Colt out of my jacket pocket and stuck it in my belt, over to the left, out of sight.

As I munched chicken and washed it down with ale, I wondered about those film cans. Not all of them, of course. I already had a pretty fair idea of the film that Marie, Judy, and Olga had made, *Sweet Life,* because I'd known all three of the girls intimately. But I was curious about the others—not so much *Danse du Ventre,* for the difference between Athena dancing naked and Athena in her dance costume couldn't be that great. Besides, I'd seen the nude still that Jock had carried in his wallet. As for *Pickup on Swing Street,* it didn't seem right to be looking at Hub and Mady's *souvenir d'amour,* as they'd called it. And as for *The Champ,* who'd want to watch Canvasback Grande and Honey Wing balling? Not I.

But *The Kama Sutra Tango?* I was toying with the idea of taking that one down to Jock's studio and running it off. Why not? It had been intended for the art theaters, and supposedly it might have won at Cannes. But then I realized this was not the time for indulging erotic fancies.

Father Vito arrived first, around ten-thirty, with Vickie and Athena. When I'd related the shoot-out on the Port Authority parking roof, Vickie didn't seem much impressed by my story of rooftop gunplay. Nor did Athena. Of course, both girls had been through a lot of heavy emotion lately. They didn't have much energy left. Athena said nothing, but simply went to the bar and fixed herself and Vickie a couple of tall Scotch and sodas. I gave Vito a cognac and had another for myself. I wondered

177

about Athena in the coming confrontation.

Her face was as impassive as an Egyptian mask. The blue eyes were deep wells of cold light.

Maginnis arrived at exactly eleven. He made his proper hellos, but he seemed a little disappointed at seeing so many people. He could hardly kill me in front of three witnesses. He'd have to waste the whole room.

Three minutes behind Maginnis, the three girls from the Bon Bon Bar and Phil Tramontana arrived. All four were speeding. They had that look, eyes darting nervously, faces flushed. Also they were uptight about Maginnis. Everyone was doing a lot of heavy breathing. I've seen scared hookers. These were terrified. Near panic. I wondered what in hell was keeping Sergeant Sweeney. I talked, filling in the time, saying nothing, vamping. Sweeney arrived at exactly ten minutes after eleven with four uniformed cops. Maginnis, Tramontana, and the girls looked ready to run, but there was no way out. Sweeney greeted Maginnis like a brother officer, then took me aside. He told me the score on the Port Authority war games: Volos dead, Rocco wounded.

"I owe you," he said. "That was quite a collar. Only Rocco isn't hurt bad. I got all kinds of charges on him, but he'll be able to lay off some of it on Volos, seeing that Volos can't talk back, so Rocco won't spend a day in jail after he gets out of the hospital. I thought you'd like to know in case you had anything to do with what happened back there on the roof."

I thanked him and we turned to the assembled guests. Show time. I made a speech, delivering the facts of the case as I'd got them from Gentleman John Volos, with two witnesses.

Maginnis looked at my two witnesses. I don't see how

178

anyone could have looked at Vickie or Athena the way he did. Pure hatred. His right hand twitched, itching for his gun.

Sergeant Sweeney asked Vickie and Athena if they attested to my relation of the story as told by Volos. They said they did. Volos had indeed said he'd given the contract to Lieutenant Maginnis, five thousand in advance, five to be paid later.

There it was, out in the open. What could Maginnis do? Well, one thing, he could rat out. Which of course he did. He stated that he'd subcontracted the Alfieri hit to Phil Tramontana.

And here was Tramontana himself to confirm or deny. It was the Year of the Rat. He admitted that he'd taken money from Maginnis for the hit, but claimed he'd only got one thousand. One from five is still four, so now everybody knew Maginnis had bought Tramontana cheap. These people reminded me of the fable of the Scorpion and the Frog. The Scorpion asked the Frog to ferry him across the pond. The Frog said he was afraid the Scorpion would sting him, and the Scorpion promised he wouldn't do that to a friend. So the Frog told him to climb on, and he started swimming across the pond with the Scorpion on his back. Halfway across, the Scorpion stung him. As the Frog began to sink, he looked up at the Scorpion and asked, "Why?" And the Scorpion smiled and said, "It's my nature."

And now Tramontana was saying that although he'd accepted one thousand from Maginnis for the Alfieri hit, he hadn't done the job himself. He'd used Marie, Judy, and Olga. Honor among thieves? Forget it. And whatever happened to the myth of the Honest Whore? Gone with the wind and the flowers. If the girls hadn't been so drugged—on meth, or coke, or whatnot—they'd have jumped him then. All three had their fingers hooked like claws. Their eyes were wild.

I asked them how much he'd paid them, and Marie cursed and said a hundred each. So now we had an Irish scorpion, Mike Maginnis, and an Italian scorpion, Phil Tramontana. And three little frogs.

I asked Tramontana why he'd subcontracted the hit to three topless dancers, and he said because they'd do it cheap since they had a personal grudge against Jock Alfieri, who had used their services in making *Sweet Life* and some loops and never paid them.

"Besides," he said, "it wasn't their first time out. These broads done a few jobs before."

"For you?" I asked.

"For themselves," he said.

Olga screamed obscenities. There are hookers walking Times Square or shaking it in the topless bars who have done a few homicides with razors, knives, even guns. They'll kill a dumper if they can, a straight john if they have to. Or for money. Or even just for the hell of it.

But there was still the question of *which* girl made the hit. Sweeney asked the question.

"Which one of you used the gun?"

He looked at Marie and Judy and Olga, and they stared back at him, eyes burning the cop down, all the while smiling their unsmiling smiles.

I said, "Maginnis knows. Ask him."

I watched Maginnis. He looked ready for anything. And of course I watched the three girls, any one of whom could have worn the male disguise, the black rat's-tail mustache, goatee, and sideburns, and the sharp suit, broad-brimmed hat, and big pink sunglasses. But only one of them had come down the patio fire escape, shot Jock, and climbed up again.

If they didn't rat on each other, the charge would still be conspiracy to commit murder, which is murder one, and they would all draw very long prison sentences. How much better, then, to turn over the one who actually used the gun. The two who ratted might draw shorter terms. And so Marie and Judy offed it on Olga, who of course denied having done it. Her word against theirs.

I had a hunch. I remembered seeing Marie and Judy dancing, or whatever they were doing, when I went to see Tramontana at the Bon Bon, but Olga had not been dancing. She'd been waiting tables. Not in bikini or leotard, but slacks. And she seemed to be favoring one leg today.

I grabbed her by the arm and twisted it behind her back so I could hold her more or less steady while I pulled off her slacks. She struggled and cursed, but I yanked at the side, splitting the zipper, pulled them down over her lovely little tush, and let them drop around her ankles. She wore scanty panties with a full-blown pink rose tacked to the crotch. She also wore a large Band-Aid on her thigh.

As I ripped off the adhesive she screamed bloody murder, and I'm sure it hurt like hell because the bandage had become stuck to the bite of a large dog, a full set of tooth marks embedded in the tender flesh of her thigh.

"You shot my dog," I said.

Olga said, "Well, the goddamn bitch bit me!"

"Since you handled the gun," I told her, "we can assume you also shot Jock, and with *my* gun, which was a very funny practical joke. My own piece. I'm still laughing."

I pulled up her pants and pushed her away from me.

181

"Yeah," she said, "I thought it was pretty funny myself. So laugh at *this*, buster!"

She had a gun in her hand. While I'd been pulling up this pretty blond murderess's pants, she was dipping my shoulder holster and copping Jock's busted Miroku. The speed-freak eyes were insane. Sergeant Sweeney and his cops began reaching for their guns. So did Maginnis.

Olga tried to squeeze off a shot at belly range, but of course the firing pin was broken and she only got a click. Before she could click again, a second gun roared and Olga was falling backward with a look of total surprise in her big brown eyes and a small fountain of blood welling from her neck where Vickie's little Astra .25 had severed her jugular. Sweeney was shouting something about everybody dropping their guns. Nobody did.

Vickie wasn't holding the gun. Athena held it, and now she turned it on Tramontana. She must have learned to shoot from a military instructor, for she used the classic technique taught in military organizations all over the world: body erect and profiled to the target, gun arm straight out with elbow slightly bent. And the range was optimal for a short-barreled automatic. One shot had taken Olga out.

Athena's second shot caught Tramontana behind the left ear. He'd been trying to duck out of the way when she nailed him. Maybe the Cobra that I'd taken off him was his only piece.

Maginnis saw which way it was going and sighted in on Athena, but she put one of those little .25-caliber pellets in his chest while he was squeezing off his shot. She missed his heart apparently, for he had time to crank one off and it caught her just under the breastbone with dum-dum impact, smack in the solar plexus, knocking her wind out, bending her double, and flinging her on her back.

It was anybody's ball game now, so I took Big Augie's big Colt out of my belt and pegged a .45-caliber copper-jacketed lead slug at Maginnis and he caught it beautifully, just under his left eye. It came out bigger than a baseball when it emerged from the back of his head. Funny thing: Maginnis had a lot of brains. When the shooting stopped, Sweeney and his cops hadn't fired a shot. How could they? They couldn't have known whom to shoot first.

The shooting stopped at this point because nobody present, and still alive, had any reason to shoot anybody else. I wasn't about to kill Marie and Judy for having been Olga's accomplices in murdering Jock and Schatzi. Death is no revenge. I only wanted to give them some time to think it over, say twenty years to life.

Father Vito got busy giving last rites. There wasn't a spark of life in Maginnis, Tramontana, or Olga. He tried Athena. He got to her just before the death rattle. I knelt by Vito and said a "Hail, Mary" and a "Hail, Holy Queen" for her Egyptian soul.

As rotten as Jock had turned out, Athena had loved him. I could understand how she'd wanted to kill whoever murdered her lover. I think I'd want to do the same, but not for a business partner, and not for a dog. I certainly wouldn't shoot a woman over a dog. Man and boy, I've known a lot of crazy broads all over the world, among them a few snowbirds and speed freaks, so the brown-eyed, natural-blond Olga Herasimchuk was not the only crazy twitch who ever tried to kill me. If it hadn't been for Jock's busted Miroku she'd have done it, too. And that's what I call poetic justice.

Vickie and I promised Sergeant Sweeney that we'd

come down to the station in the morning and make our depositions. I turned over the guns to Sweeney, except the Colt Cobra that I'd taken off Phil Tramontana. Who knows? I might need it. When everybody had gone— Sweeney and his men, the morgue attendants, the forensics detectives, and Father Vito—we set to work cleaning up the apartment. There was a lot of blood.

I thought about the future. Vickie would be going back to her ballet company in Chicago in a few days. I'd have to face Uncle Rocco when he came out of the hospital. I wondered if I should try to handle Rocco at all. Maybe I'd cut out for Amsterdam, sell a few diamonds, head for the Riviera or someplace. But first to bed. Vickie and I.

Sometime before dawn, I'd been dozing and dreaming, when Vickie nudged me in the ribs.

"Joe?" she whispered. "Did you look at any of those movies?"

I said, "No. Why?"

She said, "You know, being a dancer, and all—the movie the Garay twins made, *The Kama Sutra Tango* . . . ?"

"What about it?"

"Well, I've been wondering how they did all those *Kama Sutra* positions while dancing."

"You know how, Vickie. You've seen them dance at the club."

"Yes, but not in the nude, Joe. Do you suppose they really—you know . . . ?"

I said, "Shall we dance?"

"Have you got any tango records?"

We got up, just as we were, and went into the parlor, and I put a tango on the record player.

And we danced.

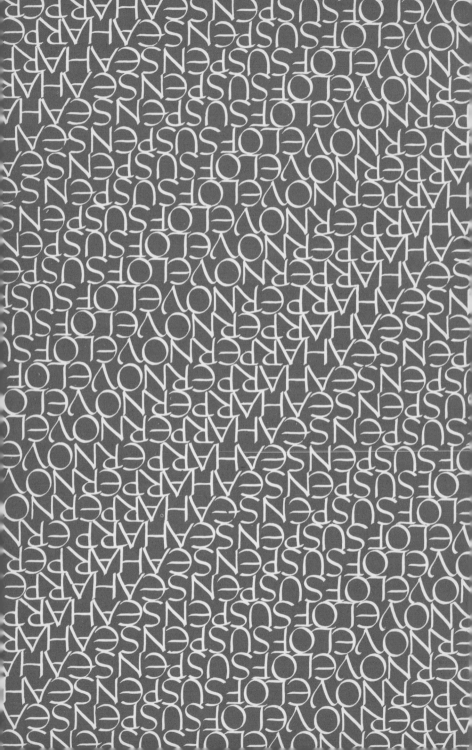